the
Master of
Wisdom

Jeanne K. Norweb

Katewood Books

In loving memory
of my dear brothers,
Henry and Bert

Katewood Books
26 Harmony School Rd.
Flemington, NJ 08822

First Printing, 2006
Printed in the United States of America

SAPH

CONTENTS

the
Master of
Wisdom

CHAPTER 1
Beyond the Door

Gregory Hartland carried a large box from the car into their new home and slammed it down, saying angrily, "What a rotten place this is . . . a perfect hole . . . and we have to live here."

"Oh, stop it," said his sister Marilyn, coming in behind him with another box. "You've been doing nothing but grumbling and complaining all day. Here, give me a hand with this; it's heavy."

Her brother did not move. "Dump it in the corner," was his sullen answer.

"Indeed I won't," she retorted. "These are Mother's big stoneware vases. She would feel badly if they were broken."

"Oh!" he said in a different tone. Their mother was slowly recovering from a serious illness. He took the box and put it carefully in a corner. Then he vented his feelings by kicking another carton marked "Books" and resumed his complaining.

"Do stop it, Greg," his sister repeated with an anxious glance towards the open door. Their parents were unpacking and she was afraid they would hear him. "You've always liked coming here before. And when Dad decided he could easily get to his new work from here, you were the one who was most enthusiastic about moving. You said you could start learning to be a doctor by going with Uncle Jack on some of his rounds."

"Well, I don't want to be a doctor now, certainly not a small country doctor living in a seaside village. If I did become a doctor, I'd be an important specialist with a big office and regular office hours. No running all over the place at any time of day or night for me!"

Marilyn checked a retort. She knew there was no use reminding him that until this year one of the reasons he so greatly admired their uncle doctor was because he had given up a well-paying city practice, as he felt he could do more good as a country doctor.

Instead she looked thoughtfully at him. They were twins, but no stranger would have guessed it. Greg was tall for his fourteen years and had brown hair and eyes, while Marilyn, or Lyn as she was usually called, was of medium height with dark blonde hair and hazel eyes. Even their temperaments were different. Greg was argumentative to the point of pugnaciousness while Lyn was quieter, liked books better than he did and was a peacemaker. She had to be. Nevertheless they understood each other and got on well together. So Lyn changed her tactics.

"After all, it's only for a year, and the doctor said the sea air would probably do wonders for Mother. Besides, Uncle Jack can keep an eye on her."

Greg was temporarily silenced. Hoping to get him in a better mood, Lyn continued while burrowing into a box she had opened, "Just think what fun we'll have this summer! I'm going to work hard at becoming a really good swimmer."

4

That was the wrong remark to make. It started Greg off again.

"Fun! You'll have all the fun. I have to have a tutor this summer. And what kind of tutor would there ever be in this dead place?"

"Well, it's your own fault that you have to be tutored," remarked their Uncle Jack who came into the room in time to hear this complaint. "You've only yourself to blame. You have plenty of brains, yet you failed your exams for your new school. It's only because my brother-in-law is Head that you are going to have another chance before school starts. I only hope you didn't fail them on purpose, hoping to be sent back to the school your parents took you out of." As this was exactly what Greg had done, he kept quiet.

His former school had been a good one, but in the past year it had greatly changed. A new headmaster had brought in all sorts of advanced ideas, as he called them. Religion classes had been eliminated as out-of-date. Teachers considered old-fashioned were quietly retired. Scientific explanations were given for everything. Gregory had come under the influence of a dynamic new teacher who considered the Bible "an antiquated collection of myths belonging to a primitive people." Science, he said, was clearing the modern mind of such foolishness, and intelligent persons of today could only believe what was scientifically proved.

Due to his mother's long illness and his father having been frequently away on business, his parents had not become aware of Greg's changed attitude toward many of the beliefs they held most im-

5

portant until nearly the end of the school year. Despite his angry protests, they had at once transferred him to another school whose exams, as his uncle suspected, he had deliberately failed, hoping in that way to force his parents to send him back to the old school, only to find that he had brought upon himself the disagreeable prospect of spending his holidays being tutored.

So Gregory Hartland started the summer in a bad mood. It improved when he discovered the tutor was as enthusiastic about soccer as he was. Nevertheless, to show he would think as he pleased, he paraded his new theories as often as possible and pooh-poohed any idea he thought old-fashioned.

"Religion's all right for girls," he commented loftily one Sunday as they were coming out of church, which he unwillingly attended, "but I'm going to join the Air Force, and fighting men don't need religion."

"So you think fighting men don't have any religion," came a stern voice from behind him. It was Captain Manley, a retired naval officer who was a friend of their uncle. "You've a great deal to learn, my boy, and you had better learn it fast."

He strode off, saying to the huge black Newfoundland dog who was waiting for him, "Admiral Drake, what that cocksure youngster needs is a visit to Smuggler's Cove at the right time."

"Wonder why he said that?" Greg said to Lyn.

"Said what?" She hadn't heard the Captain's remark.

Greg repeated it and added, annoyed but curious, "I wonder where Smuggler's Cove is, though he's probably senile and doesn't know what he's talking about."

"He isn't senile and knows perfectly well what he's talking about," Lyn answered indignantly. "I met him the other day at Uncle Jack's. You should hear the interesting stories he tells about all the places he's been."

"Well, saying I should go to see a cove sounds pretty senile to me."

Lyn ignored his remark. "Let's find out about the cove."

They asked several people but all they got was a vague, "It's up the coast somewhere." So they forgot about it, until a couple of weeks later. Then, Lyn remembered it when they were down at the wharf talking to a fisherman they had made friends with.

"That's an old cove, just a little way up the coast. Long ago it was used by smugglers because, except at low tide, it can only be reached by boat or by a pretty steep climb down the cliffs. There's a cave where the smugglers hid their goods until it was picked up by their partners."

Lyn was excited. "A real smuggler's cave! I'd love to see it!"

"How do we get there?" Greg asked.

"Tide's nearly out now," said the fisherman. "If you want to come upon it by boat the way the smugglers did, you can borrow that small rowboat of mine there. It's the green one. The cove's not far. You can't miss it, as the rocks stick out into the sea on both sides like arms and you can see the cave from the sea."

"Let's get some buns from the bakery and make

an afternoon of it," Lyn suggested.

They had a brief tiff over who would pay for the buns.

"It's your turn to treat," Lyn insisted.

"No, it's yours. Besides, I've spent almost all of my pocket money."

"I need mine for a book I've been wanting for ages. In fact, I'm going to buy it this afternoon." She patted her purse through the pocket of her shorts.

Lyn was not selfish by nature but she had a very strong sense of possession; besides, she wanted that particular book very badly. In the end they shared the cost of the buns.

"All right. I'll dash top speed and get the buns."

Lyn laughed. "If you're going to dash top speed, I'll wait here. You'd be back before I was halfway there."

Greg had won prizes at school for sprinting and she knew it was hopeless for her to try to keep up with him.

While waiting for Greg, Lyn bailed some rain water out of the rowboat, then sat watching the sea. Too bad all the lands of Earth have been discovered, she thought with regret. In the old days, each time the mariners set sail on a voyage of discovery they must have felt they were taking an unknown road.

Greg came tearing back with the buns and climbed into the boat. They each took an oar and began rowing. Both were wearing light jackets, as the day was chilly; but rowing was hard work and they soon got so hot, they stopped to take them off.

"Don't lay your jacket down anywhere, or else it will have the same fishy smell as this boat," said

Lyn, tying hers by the sleeves around her neck. Greg did the same with his. They were growing tired when they at last rounded a jutting arm of rocks and saw a snug, quiet little cove.

"This must be it. There's the cave," cried Lyn, looking over her shoulder as they rowed in. They ran the boat aground, jumped out and dragged the boat well up onto the sand. They were about to look in the cave when another boy and girl about their own age came around the other jutting arm of rocks, walking on the wet sand left by the tide. They were carrying a basket.

"Hello!" said the boy. "Are you going to picnic here?"

"No," answered Lyn. "We just rowed in to see the cave. We'll be leaving in a moment."

Greg didn't remember seeing them in town. "Do you live here?" he asked.

"No," said the other boy. "We both live outside of Bath. We came to visit our grandfather, Captain Manley. I'm David Manley and this is my cousin, Laura Manley."

Greg and Lyn introduced themselves, then Lyn walked over to the cave and looked in. It was not large and she could take it in at a glance. She called back casually over her shoulder, "Where does that door lead to?"

To her surprise, Laura and David yelled, "What!" and both raced into the cave, only to stop short and say disappointedly, "There's no door."

Lyn thought they were making fun of her and said crossly, "Of course there is. Don't try to pull my leg. I'm not that stupid."

"Do you *really* see a door?" said Laura wistfully.

"Of course she does!" exclaimed Greg angrily. "I do, too! What do you mean by saying you don't see a door? It's right in front of your noses!"

"No, I really don't see it," said Laura sadly.

"Nor do I," said David. He sounded just as sad as the girl.

"Do you think we're lying?" shouted Lyn, stamping her foot impatiently.

"No," answered Laura. "I'm sure the door is there. It's just that we can't see it anymore." She sounded even sadder. "But we did once . . . three times, really."

"It means, Laura," said David, "they're the ones who are meant to go through it this time. We gave up our chance to go back."

"What on earth are you talking about?" demanded Greg. "Do you mean you really can't see a big wooden door?"

"A wooden door with a rounded top and no handle. It's a swinging door," said David. He saw Lyn and Greg were staring at him in complete bewilderment. "Look here. We believe you see it, and you've got to believe Laura and I don't. No, don't try opening it yet," he continued, catching hold of Greg's arm as he started towards the door. "Wait a moment, and we'll tell you about it."

His earnestness impressed both Lyn and Greg. Obviously, there was something strange about this door.

"I warn you," David went on. "You're going to have a hard time swallowing our story. You'll have to believe in dragons."

"Dragons?" said Lyn dubiously. "They belong in fairy tales and we're pretty old for that sort of thing."

"Yes, dragons. And another world just beyond that door."

"Beyond that door!" exclaimed Greg skeptically. "I don't think that's scientifically possible."

"Probably not. But it's there and so are the dragons. Sit down and listen to us; then you can open the door."

They sat down on the sand. Laura and David told Lyn and Greg about their three visits to the land of the Green Dragons, the dragons who all wore a gold armband in pledge that they would keep the laws of the Great One. And of the Blue Road. As she listened to their description of the Blue Road, which the faithful dragons at the end of their lives took Home, Lyn felt a tremendous longing to see it, while Greg tried hard to say "Bosh" and couldn't. They heard about the young Prince Nimeon who had become a great King and had sacrificed himself to save his people from the dreaded Sea Serpent.

"We can't go there anymore," and again Laura sounded sorrowful, but this time Lyn understood why. "We gave it up. That's why we can't see the door. But since you can, it's there for you. You're meant to open it."

Greg got up suddenly and pushed open the door, still half doubting, and stared as the door opened onto a sunlit glade covered with deep green grass, dotted with bright flowers and surrounded by magnificent trees. He caught his breath.

11

"Come on, Lyn!" he cried. "It really *is* there! Oh, come on!" But Lyn was already beside him, staring wide-eyed.

"Are you certain we can get back?" she asked breathlessly. "And will the time really be the same here no matter how long we stay?"

"Yes, yes," cried Laura. "And be sure to tell the dragons you're friends of ours, the Laura and David who were named Friends of the King Forever by their great King Nimeon. I'm sure they'll give you a grand welcome. Dragons don't forget. We're in their stories."

But Greg and Lyn had vanished and she was speaking to the rocky wall of the cave.

As the twins stepped through the door it swung shut behind them and they found themselves standing in the glade.

"The land of the Green Dragons," said Lyn wonderingly. "How much bluer their sky is than ours."

"And look at the size of those trees. Nothing like it at home. But come on," said her brother leading the way through the trees. "This is the direction David said to take."

"Hope the dragons are as friendly as they used to be. What shall we say to the first one we meet? Remember, we must be extremely polite," Lyn cautioned.

They decided as they walked along that the safest plan would be to follow Laura's advice and explain at once they were friends of Laura and David and ask to be taken to the King.

"On the back of a dragon?" said Lyn doubtfully. "Though I must say it did sound like fun."

"Of course," Greg replied. "They went everywhere on Nimeon's back. Planes must seem tame after riding on the back of a dragon."

They walked on through the forest, looking around them, but all they could see were trees. Except for the occasional alarm cry of a bird, there was no sound. The trees ended at a large meadow through which flowed a broad, lazy river dotted here and there with a water plant whose blossoms were like huge yellow and white chrysanthemums. They walked along its banks through the meadow, watching the sky for any sign of dragons. The sun was directly overhead and it was very hot. This was the time of day when the dragons usually rested, but the children did not know that and began to think the dragons might now be extinct.

"Let's sit down for a while under this clump of trees until it cools off a little," said Lyn.

As they went around to the shady side, she stepped on the tail of a dragon who was snoozing peacefully in the shade. The dragon reared up, blowing out smoke wrathfully. Lyn screamed.

"Who are you? And what do you mean by stepping on my tail?" The children were frozen to the spot. It is one thing to talk happily about friendly dragons, and quite another to meet one, especially an angry dragon whose tail you have stepped on.

Greg's mouth was so dry he felt his tongue was glued to the roof of it, but he managed to bow and stammer, "We're Friends of the King. I mean, we're friends of Laura and David who were named Friends of the King Forever by your great King Nimeon."

The dragon snorted, this time blowing out fire as well as smoke, but fortunately, not in Lyn's and Greg's direction.

"That is a likely story! Nimeon the Great, son of Manamor the Wise, lived eight reigns past. True, Laura and David were famous heroes in Nimeon's day, but they could not be alive now. Do you really expect me to believe that?"

Lyn and Greg looked at each other in complete consternation. Nothing of the glowing account they had heard of the Green Dragons had prepared them for this. Yet the dragon did fit David's description of them. All the dragons, he said, were green, but the dragonesses had silver markings and the dragons gold markings. This one was evidently a dragon and he wore the gold armband on his right foreleg.

Lyn, remembering Laura's emphasis on how much the dragons valued politeness, bowed and said in as firm a voice as she could manage under the frightening circumstances, "I beg your pardon for stepping on your tail. It was an accident. If you want, we'll go right back to where we came from, or else, could we please go to your King?"

The dragon snorted again, but less violently.

"Of course you are going to the King. I am taking you there right now. His Majesty will decide what is to be done with you." He spread his great wings.

"May we ride on your back," Greg asked politely, "the way Laura and David rode on King Nimeon?"

This time the dragon gave such a snort that flames several feet long shot out. "A warrior never exposes his back to someone who might be an enemy."

He sat back on his haunches and reached towards them. His talons looked enormous.

"Please, oh please, don't hurt us," begged Lyn. She was trembling so hard she could barely stand.

The dragon paused, then bent down his head and looked at them closely. "Do not worry," he said in a much less gruff voice. "I am not going to."

And with that he caught hold of them and swept upwards.

He was right, he did not hurt them, but his clutch was very uncomfortable. His talons were clasped around their waists so they were hanging sideways. Luckily it was only a short flight to the palace. Lyn and Greg got a confused glimpse of a huge stone building before they were ignominiously dumped in a courtyard with trees on one side under which several dragons were lounging.

"Grand welcome! My hat!" exclaimed Greg as he picked himself up from the pavement and helped Lyn to her feet.

"I found these strangers and have brought them to the King," their dragon captor was saying to one of the others. "They say they come from that place Earth where the famous Laura and David of the old tales came from."

"Their Majesties have gone to a wedding," said the other dragon, "and are not expected back until sunset. Their Highnesses have gone with them, and so has our Captain. So you will have to wait until His Majesty gets back."

He came over and asked, "Are you really from

Earth as in the old tales?"

"Yes, we are," replied Greg hopefully.

"Well, well, His Majesty will have to decide about that," the dragon said in a not unfriendly voice. He motioned towards an archway. "You can stay in there out of the sun until he comes back."

They went through the doorway into a cool stone room. It was a relief to be out of the hot sun and they cheered up a little.

"After all, they've not tried to harm us yet," commented Lyn. "And we did wake him suddenly from his sleep. He could have swallowed us in one mouthful."

"Or more likely roasted us in one breath," Greg said feelingly. He looked around. "What a huge room this is. Wonder what it is used for?"

It was a large room in Earth's measurements with a very high ceiling. Actually, it was a small storeroom, but they were not yet used to dragon-size rooms. Against one wall was a very solid table and several chests, and along another were piled big baskets.

"Are we prisoners?" asked Lyn.

"Well, I wouldn't try to make a bolt for freedom." Greg went over to a chest, climbed up, and looked out of the window above it. "The dragons look asleep but I wouldn't count on it. I suspect they can move fast when they want to, and it would just irritate them. They might throw us into a dungeon."

Lyn climbed up beside him. The dragons did indeed look comfortable, asleep in the shade of the huge trees. Even their captor was settling down to finish his snooze. There was also a lizard-like animal about ten feet long who evidently liked the heat as he was lying on the hot pavement in full sun.

"That must be one of the Dragon-Cousins," said Lyn, leaning out and looking around. The scene made her think of people on Earth sitting on park benches on a summer day. She felt better. "I think they are going to be just as nice as Laura and David said they were."

"I hope so." Greg's tone was dubious.

They grew thirsty. Greg peered out the door. "I wonder if we dare ask for some water?"

Lyn pulled him back. "Wait, they are bound to wake up soon."

But it seemed a long time before the dragons began to move around. At last the Dragon-Cousin woke up, stretched, and crawled past their window. He didn't look as fierce as the dragons, so Greg ventured to ask, "Could we have a drink of water, please?"

"Certainly, I will bring you some."

He crawled off and was soon back with two good-sized bowls balanced on his back. The water was deliciously cool, and after they had finished drinking, they washed their hands and faces and felt very refreshed. The Dragon-Cousin was more talkative than the dragons and told them his name was Katanga, and asked how they had come to the land of the Green Dragons. When they told him about the Door, he glanced at them sharply with new interest. "Through the Forbidden Door, hmmm, perhaps . . . perhaps . . . " and fell silent.

"Perhaps what?" Lyn asked. "Is it really forbidden for you to open the Door, even though it's there all the time, and not just every now and then as with us?"

"Yes," answered Katanga. "Except for the one time when Nimeon the Great opened it to save his disobedient friend, some evil has come upon the kingdom when one of us on this side has opened it."

He was very willing to answer their other questions. Yes, Their Majesties would surely be back by sunset. The whole royal family had gone because it was such an important wedding. The Captain of the Border Guard's youngest daughter was marrying the grandson of the First Councillor. Both the King and Queen were wearing their second-best jeweled collars. They were not as magnificent as the Coronation ones, of course, but were very beautiful nevertheless. "Get a good look at them. My people made them generations uncounted previously."

"How many are there in the royal family?" was Lyn's next question.

"Their Majesties, Prince Damor and Princess Edrina. There is another little Prince, but he is only a passing old and sickly."

"Passing, passing . . . what's that?" asked Greg.

Lyn poked him and whispered, "Remember? It's what they call a year."

A dragon came over and asked Katanga if the Queen's brother had gone with the King.

"Catch either the Councillor or the Captain asking *him*, or Wondan either," retorted Katanga. "It was an evil day for the land of the Green Dragons when His Majesty let that dark enemy not only come to this land but actually live in the palace. The

18

Dark Dragons come and go as they have never been allowed to do before. I think they are spying on the land."

Several dragons nodded their heads in agreement.

"Wondan is not so bad," commented one of the younger dragons lazily. "And some of the Dark Dragonesses are charming."

"I do not trust anyone who does not wear the gold armband," grunted the Dragon-Cousin.

"Why?" said Lyn.

"We wear the armband as a pledge of our allegiance to the Great One and His laws. The Dark Dragons mock us for this and they scorn the Blue Road. Or so they say. Personally, I think they fear it.

"Have you ever asked one of your 'charming Dark Dragonesses' to go with you to the Blue Road?" he continued, addressing the young dragon who had admired them.

The dragon appeared startled. "No," he said thoughtfully. "No, I have not."

"Try it and see what happens. None will go with you." Leaving the dragon to think over what he had said, Katanga turned again to the children.

"The dark Wondan wishes to marry our Princess," said one of the dragons. Even the younger dragons were angry at this remark and showed it by blowing out smoke and flames. "How dare he?" "The impudence of him." "The Princess never speaks to him if she can avoid it," were some of the angry comments.

"Who is Wondan?" Lyn asked, surprised at the dragons' reactions.

"He is a Dark Dragon whom our King allows to stay at the palace though he does not wear the armband. That, at least, His Majesty will not permit," explained Katanga.

"Dark Dragons living here!" Greg exclaimed in astonishment. "Why, I thought they were your enemies because they want to conquer you and take over your country!"

"That is true . . ." the Dragon-Cousin began in a grim voice, but was interrupted by another Dragon-Cousin who came scurrying out of the palace, calling:

"Katanga! Katanga! Come quickly, one of my children has cut his foot badly and needs your skill."

Katanga at once followed her into the palace and the children were again left to themselves.

"Sounds as though something were wrong here," Lyn whispered to her brother. "Did you notice the warning looks those two dragons over there gave Katanga?"

Greg nodded. "And then the grim looks they gave each other." Neither felt enough at ease with the dragons to continue asking questions, and the dragons paid no further attention to them.

After a while, though, Greg got up courage and asked their captor if they could look around.

"Yes, but you must stay within the courtyard."

They walked about and peered through doorways, but nobody was there and they all seemed to open onto passageways or empty rooms. Once, they took a few steps from the pavement in order to look around a corner and were immediately told to go back, even though no dragon appeared to be watching them. "They must have eyes in the back of their heads," said Greg as they hastily ran back.

There were no such things as benches so they finally sat down on the stones with their backs against the shady side of the building.

The longer the shadows grew, the hungrier and more apprehensive they became. From where they sat they could see the highest of the two square towers on which, Katanga had told them, was stationed a sentinel, adding, "When Their Majesties come in sight, he will give a warning call, and then at his second call the guards on duty will come to attention."

They were both watching so intently that they were startled when a harsh voice said, "Well, so these are the prisoners."

In one of the doorways was a large black dragon with a grey chest and sharp, small black and yellow eyes. He did not have an armband as did all the other dragons. Lyn and Greg jumped up. They had been afraid of the fire-blowing green warrior they had stumbled over under the trees, but not like this. There was something hard and cruel in this one's gaze and they instinctively retreated towards the Green Dragons.

"I will take them with me," continued the Dark Dragon. "Come," he said sharply to them.

They were relieved when their captor said vigorously, "No, they are my prisoners and I am taking them to the King."

The Dark Dragon breathed out smoke wrathfully but before he could say anything further, a cry came from the tower: "Their Majesties!"

"Come with me," said their captor and they gladly followed him, suddenly feeling he was a refuge.

Half walking, half gliding, he moved so quickly they had to trot to keep up with him. He led them around the outer wall of the palace until he came to a wide stone terrace with a broad expanse of rough lawn dotted with immense trees in front of it. At one end of the terrace he stopped and waited.

CHAPTER 2
The Crippled King

A second call rang out from the tower. The guards on duty at once flew up at attention. Never in all their lives would Greg or Lyn ever forget their first view of dragons in flight. Three of the warriors were lined up opposite the other three. Their heads were all held exactly at the same angle, their tails were curved alike and, as they hovered in place, their huge wings moved slowly up and down in perfect unison. At each beat, their gold markings gleamed in the last rays of the setting sun. Then black against the red and yellow sky came six dragons flying two-by-two. As they passed the guard, each pair acknowledged the salute with a slight bow of their heads. Above the lawn, the first dragon wheeled and started to slowly circle down. No one needed to tell the children, this was the King. There was something grand and regal in his every movement. The Queen followed closely after him and then the other four, until all were circling down in the same spiral. Six great black silhouettes glinting now light, now dark, in the setting sun as they slowly wheeled.

One by one they landed on the terrace, three dragons and three dragonesses. All, of course, wore the gold armband. As soon as they were down, the waiting warrior went forward and saluted, which means a special quick bow of the head straight up and down, and asked permission to speak. It was granted and the warrior motioned Lyn and Greg forward, then told the King about their capture.

"And Sire," he ended indignantly, "they expected me to believe they know the Laura and David who came here in the days of Nimeon the Great!"

Greg looked anxiously at the King who showed neither surprise nor indignation. All he said was, "It is possible. Time runs at different speeds in different worlds." He looked at Lyn and Greg. "Leave them here."

The dragon saluted and flew off, shooting straight up into the air, warrior style. The warriors always take off in that manner and land fast, dropping with wings closed. It is only when they are with dragonesses or children that they circle down.

Lyn had been staring at the King's and Queen's magnificent collars which were dazzling because of the size and brilliance of the jewels. The King's was especially striking because of the predominance of rubies in it. "Our Crown Jewels are nothing like these, and if these are only second best, what must the best be like," she thought. The next pair of dragons who seemed considerably younger wore plain heavy gold chains around their necks. Undoubtedly, these were Prince Damor and Princess Edrina. The last pair had no ornaments and were wrinkled and elderly looking. Must be the Councillor and his wife whose grandson just got married, she guessed.

The King looked at them through half-closed eyes for a long time without speaking, while they tried not to fidget. At last he spoke gruffly and rest-lessly moved his left wing which seemed to not quite hang properly in place.

"You are welcome in the name of the Great One. Now tell me how and why you come here."

Immensely relieved by the King's words, Greg told him how they had met Laura and David and found the Door in the cave, but at the same time he wondered if the dragons would possibly accept such a story. He couldn't imagine anyone on Earth be-lieving it. He never would have, but the King seemed to be having no difficulty. Instead, though he appeared to be paying only perfunctory attention to what they were saying, he soon began to listen intently and so did the other dragons. The Prince, who lay beside the Queen, never took his eyes off them, except every now and then to glance at his father.

When Greg repeated Laura's words that the Door was there for them alone and for a special rea-son, the King nodded his head gravely and again was silent for a long time. At last he said, "Yes, surely there is a reason the Forbidden Door was there for you to open, but not only a reason for you, but for us also; for that is how the tales run that I have been calling to mind."

"Surely, Your Majesty, just for them," came a new voice. It struck Greg as a very smooth voice. Two more dragons had come out of the palace: one was green, with an armband, and the other was the Dark Dragon who had tried to get hold of them in the courtyard. They both looked at the children with unfriendly eyes.

"No," replied the King slowly and thoughtfully. "The Door has two sides, theirs and ours. Ours is always here and we well know that evil will come upon us when it is opened; but it is not so with their side. There is a reason for them and for us, and somewhere those reasons will meet and be one. I must think of this and consult the Master of Wisdom." He made a movement as if to fly off. Lyn saw the Prince and Princess glance quickly at each other.

"Your Majesty is very wise," the smooth-voiced dragon continued. "But surely tomorrow will be enough time, for Your Majesty has flown far this day. Is that not so, my sister?" he said, addressing the Queen at these last words. She nodded nervously but did not speak. "Or let me go in Your Majesty's stead," he ended in a tone of unctuous concern.

"Do you dare to think you could take the King's place in such an important matter as this?" the Princess asserted.

The dragon started to protest, but the King interrupted him, saying resolutely, "The Princess is right. I am the King and shall go myself. None shall hinder me." He stared hard at the two dragons and his eyes began to glow fiercely. "For some reason, Magior, you do not wish me to go. But I have been thinking more and more these days that I have listened too much to your counsel and it has not been good for me or for my realm. Now these children come and the past tells me they come for a purpose, perhaps even a warning. I have also been thinking of late that I should never have granted your request, the Queen's brother though you be, that this

Dark Dragon live among us." Short, fiery puffs were coming from his nostrils. "My Queen, look well after these guests; I go to the Master." With a farewell bow he flew up from the terrace into the nearly dark sky. As he leapt up it was easy to see that his left wing and left back leg were stiff. Now no one could miss the black looks that the Queen's brother and Wondan gave the children. The twins edged back. Damor saw this and moved between them and the other two.

Magior blew angry puffs of smoke. "How could you let the King go out into the cold air again? His wing and leg will be worse than ever," he scolded his sister.

"How could I stop him? He would only have been angrier at you if I had tried," replied the Queen nervously. "I must see about a meal being prepared for our guests," and she vanished into the palace.

Magior followed her and so did Wondan after another threatening look.

"At last! At last!" cried the Princess triumphantly.

"Yes, at last," responded Damor, though more quietly.

The First Councillor agreed gravely. "Yes, at last the King has gone to the Master. I, too, think these Children from Earth have been sent as a sign to us in our time of need and trouble." He spread his wings for flight, then paused and, nodding towards Greg and Lyn, added, "And for this reason it would be wise to keep a close watch over them. There are those who would not want a sign."

With friendly bows of their heads, he and his wife flew off.

"He is right," the Prince said in a low voice to his sister.

Lyn was frightened. "What did he mean?" she asked anxiously, though the black looks of Magior and Wondan were, she feared, all the answer needed.

The Prince said, still in a low tone, as though afraid of being overheard, "I will tell you later; now come with me."

He entered the palace through another doorway and went down a long hall. High along the sides were torches that were being lit by a dragon by means of a quick, fiery puff.

The Prince led them to his own quarters and lit the torches himself. "Watch that no one listens," he cautioned his sister. He settled himself on the floor while she stayed near the door. In the room was a large bed of rushes, covered with hides, two chests and several baskets of different sizes with neck straps, the kind used by dragons for carrying things, and a low table. Since there was no other place to sit, Greg and Lyn hoisted themselves onto the table and sat with their legs dangling. As they did so, a voice came from the hall, "It is I, Katanga," which is the dragon equivalent of knocking.

"Come in, Katanga. Have you heard? My father has at last gone to consult the Master, for he thinks that Lyn and Greg are a portent, and so does the First Councillor," said Damor.

"Ah, that is good news indeed. I, too, feel these two are a sign. Have I not said of our King that he could still be roused from the lethargy into which he has fallen deeper and deeper these last few passings? The coming of these Children from Earth has done this. Perhaps it will do more, for he is always most a King when faced with some urgent matter. It is the small things he has always been inclined to let slip."

"But what is wrong? If they are only small things?" said Greg, surprised at the seriousness of Katanga's voice.

"What are most days filled with, if not small things?" said Damor. "At night, whether the days are full or empty, they depart never to return and never really to be forgotten. Are you not taught that?" he ended, looking at Greg curiously.

Since Greg could remember a good many days he would have liked to forget, he kept quiet.

"Now these 'small things' have become so many," the Prince went on with a deep sigh. "Whenever I have tried to point them out to my father, he says they are not important enough for a King to trouble about . . . that is what the lesser officials are for and, indeed, what they need to keep them busy. Always that . . . let others do it . . . others . . . . Sometimes my father does speak to Magior who offers to right the matter, then nothing is done or else worse follows. Even what I can do is limited by Magior's bad advice and my father's indifference." He was silent a long, long moment, then said sorrowfully and in a much lower voice, "Alas, that I, his son, should have to admit such things."

The twins were anxious to hear more explanations.

"Do you mean . . ." Greg began, but was interrupted by a voice at the door which announced the arrival of another Dragon-Cousin with dinner for the guests, sent by the Queen. There were bowls and dishes all down his head and back, but not a drop had been spilled.

Greg and Lyn jumped off the table and quickly took the dishes off, as that was evidently what they were expected to do.

"How delicious it smells!" exclaimed Lyn, appreciatively sniffing at what looked like a stew.

"And am I hungry!" was Greg's remark.

They would either have to eat standing up at the table or picnic-style on the floor. They chose the latter and were about to start when Lyn first, then Greg, noticed that the dragons and Dragon-Cousins were staring at them in surprise.

They glanced at each other, then Lyn remembered and jumped to her feet, pulling Greg up with her.

"How good of the Queen to remember us. Please tell her how grateful we are," she said in her politest voice.

Greg caught on. "Yes, and thank you for managing to get it to us so hot." He bowed awkwardly, not being used to bows.

"Anytime you wish to eat I shall be glad to bring you something; we Dragon-Cousins eat more frequently than the dragons do, so there is always something in the kitchen," was the friendly answer, and off went the server.

Fresh fruit and chunks of what must have been a mammoth loaf of some kind of bread were easy to eat, but how to tackle the stew without spoons or forks was a problem. Lyn drank the liquid part first and then scooped out the meat and vegetables with her hand, while Greg fished for the solid parts first and drank the remainder. The results were the same: their hands and faces were dripping with stew. Fortunately there was a large jar of water in the corner of the room into which they could duck their faces, and they emerged clean but very wet and had to dry themselves with their jackets which were still tied around their necks. This surprised the others immensely. They wanted to know what the jackets were for, and so Lyn gave a demonstration as to how they were used.

Neither the Prince nor Princess said anything more about their father though they and Katanga answered questions about the Green Dragons and their long enmity with the Dark Dragons, whose ways and thoughts were so different from theirs, and about the guard they kept on their border between the two kingdoms.

"Are the Dark Dragons and their ideas really so dangerous?" asked Greg. "Isn't it a good thing to let new ideas in?"

"Ways and thoughts against the laws of the Great One are never good, whether new or old, and they are never really new," said Katanga. "Besides, should the Dark Dragons ever gain control of this kingdom they would enslave us. We could not fly from them as the Green Dragons could. It is only because of the Green Dragons' vigilance that we Dragon-Cousins can live in peace."

The relationship between Katanga and the Prince

31

had been puzzling Greg as it seemed to be more that of intimate friends than that of a Prince and his subject. He looked back and forth at them so many times that Katanga finally laughed and said, "There is something you want to ask."

Greg was embarrassed at being caught off guard. He put on his most sophisticated look and said, "You seem to be such friends."

"We are," replied the Prince, "and have been for many passings. Why does that seem strange to you?"

"You are so different. Besides, you are a Prince and Katanga isn't, or perhaps he is," he added as an afterthought.

Both the Prince and Katanga laughed.

Katanga said, "The Prince is my Prince and one day, I trust, will be my King, but he is also my friend."

"There are many such friendships among us," said Damor. "My father and old Orimalgon are such friends that often he is the only one my father will listen to."

"That is so. And I must go to Orimalgon and tell him what has happened," said Katanga.

Wishing them goodnight, he was about to leave when the Princess said, "Here he is now," and called down the hall, "Orimalgon, please come here."

In a few moments the elderly Dragon-Cousin entered. The situation was explained to him and he agreed. "Yes, surely these Children from Earth have come as a sign. I shall wait for the King, no matter at what hour he returns, to tend his wing; and also, perhaps by judicious words, to help keep alive whatever advice the Master may have given him. As to the children, heed well the warning given by the Councillor and keep close watch over them and let the King see them often so that his will to do right will not falter, although . . . this time I do not think it will." He turned to the Prince. "And you, hold yourself ready for whatever shall come."

Bidding them goodnight, he and Katanga left.

A high voice called at the door. The Queen entered. "Really, Damor, if these are children from – what is that place they come from? – they should be in bed by now." Her voice and manner were as fussy as ever.

"Certainly, Dar-mother," answered the Princess as she took Lyn with her. "I told my Nurse to prepare a bed for you in my room," she told Lyn. As the Princess turned into a room a little farther down the hall she chuckled quietly.

In one corner of the room was the Princess' bed, which was also a large pile of rushes covered with several well-tanned hides. In another corner a dragoness and two Dragon-Cousins were preparing a second equally large bed.

"Is that the size of the friend who is spending the night with you?" grumbled the dragoness. "Why didn't you tell me it was not a dragoness? All this work for nothing."

"I am so sorry, Nurse," apologized Edrina. "This is Lyn who came from that strange place, Earth, that you used to tell me about when I was small."

The Nurse grumbled a little more but quickly pulled apart the nearly made bed and stuffed the extra rushes into the baskets which she balanced on the Dragon-Cousins' backs. In a few minutes she and her helpers had a small bed for Lyn comfortably piled up. They left and Lyn was going to ask more questions when the Queen came back and hovered nervously about, asking Lyn several times if there was anything more she would like to eat or drink, and was she comfortable. Did she think she would sleep well, or would she like a little potion? "I often have to take one myself when I cannot sleep for worrying about the King and our child."

Lyn assured her several times she did not need anything and at last, in desperation, hoping to encourage the Queen to leave, she curled up on her bed. She meant to chat with Edrina as soon as the Queen left, but she stayed so long telling Edrina about her worries and fears that Lyn fell asleep.

The Queen had not troubled Damor and Greg further; but though Greg would have liked to talk, as soon as his bed was made, Damor wished him goodnight and curled up without saying another word.

The next day Greg discovered that Damor took the Councillor's words of warning seriously and neither he nor Lyn were left alone for a moment; either Damor or Edrina were always with them. And, to their great disappointment, neither the Prince nor Princess showed the slightest sign of being about to fly anywhere. The twins were both dying to fly on a dragon's back.

"When I am free I will take you both," Damor promised them, "or else Edrina will, but in my father's absence I have to be on the terrace each morning for as long as is needed so that I can answer questions, give orders – in my father's name, of course – and listen to news that he might wish to hear.

"If I do not take my father's place, I have found that Magior manages to do so, but in such a way that my father is not aware he is being supplanted. Now, however, after his severe words to Magior last night, I realize he has seen more than I thought he did."

A few moments later Magior did indeed come onto the terrace and tried to persuade the Prince to leave.

"Prince Damor, how well you are learning your future duties," he said, bowing repeatedly after a Dragon-Cousin had come and gone. "But do you think that was the best answer to give just now? I think I could have helped you – only from my greater experience, of course – to give wiser advice. Anyway, as you see, few are coming, and since His Majesty has not come back to the palace, would it not be wiser for you, his son, to go to the Mount and see that all is well with him? It is so strange he has not come back; he may be ill."

"If my father is ill, then he could not be in a better place than with the Master or better tended than by him who is the best Healer in the kingdom, as you well know, and who would watch over him unceasingly."

"The Queen was so distraught over her poor son, who was coughing last night, that all she can do is hang over his crib. But should not the King's son and daughter be also watching unceasingly over their father?" Now there was a threatening note under Magior's still-courteous words. "I do not need to warn you, my dear Prince, for you are very dear to me, that your beloved father would take it very ill if he found out . . ." (seeming that he is going to tell the King, thought Greg) "that his son refused to fly to him though told that his father might be dangerously ill. He might feel, as I fear he already has reason to do, that his son soon hoped to inherit the kingdom."

"If my father thinks that, it is only because you or Wondan keep putting it into his mind. They are not my thoughts at all," said Damor; and though his voice was quiet, his eyes were beginning to glow. "I am here because as my father's son it is my duty to remain here in his place, as he himself has taught me to do. As soon as I can I will go to him."

"No one is going to take Damor's place in representing our father, the King, especially someone who is not a member of the Council," added Edrina. "Damor, stay right where you are and finish your duty. I will go at once to the Mount and explain what you are doing, and also your accusations, Magior!"

"True, I am not a member of the Council . . . at least not yet," he replied, and the threatening note was now less veiled. "But I am a trusted friend, as well as the Queen's brother, and so have great influence with both of Their Majesties. Since the King has another son, it might be well for the son who hopes to be the next King to keep me as a friend – and his daughter as well."

"Well, at least you have now declared your

true motives," said Damor, giving him a long, hard look. A dragon flew down and the Prince turned to listen to him.

"Not that we had any doubts as to your conniving," said Edrina. She turned to the children. "Come, Lyn and Greg. I will carry you to the Mount and show you the kingdom as we fly." They ran over to her, but before they could climb on her back, the Dark Dragon, Wondan, dropped down beside her.

"Ah, Princess, how beautiful you look this morning, but then, you are always beautiful. I see you are about to take off. Will you make a flight with me?"

To the children's disappointment the Princess closed her wings abruptly. "No, I am not going to fly anywhere at this moment." Then she added firmly, "Wondan, I am not interested in your attentions. Besides, the King has told you not to speak to me in this way as I am not of age."

Wondan paid no attention to her words. "Perhaps I can win your favor by taking these little friends of yours for a flight. I heard them say they wished it."

He made a movement towards Lyn who was standing near him. Remembering how the warrior had caught them up in his talons, she hastily moved to the other side of the Princess. "No . . . no, thank you," she said, not wanting to antagonize him. "Prince Damor said he would take us."

Wondan's eyes grew hard, but he said nothing and flew off with Magior, who said loudly, "Someday that young Prince will regret having spurned my friendship."

Soon afterwards Damor stretched and said he was free to go. "Come, we will go to the Master."

"Shall I come with you?" asked Edrina.

Damor thought a while. The children were beginning to realize why they had been told they would have to get used to long dragon silences. "The dragons really take their time thinking," David had said.

"No," he answered. "Dar-mother is very fond of you and likes to have you near her. That is good, for the more you are with her, the more, perhaps, you will be able to help her break free of the hold her brother has over her. Let her hear what happened this morning first from you; then if Father complains to her, she will tell him the truth."

"Yes, she will not lie. I think, though she does not dare say so, that she knows her brother's influence over the King is not good, but she fears him. Deep down, I suspect, she longs to be free of him. Several times I have found her weeping after Magior has left her."

Damor spread his wings. Lyn scrambled up in front with Greg behind her holding onto her waist, and the dragon took off.

"At last we're flying!" shouted Greg.

"It's wonderful!" Lyn shouted back. They could feel the dragon's muscles moving beneath their legs, and the breeze made by the rhythmical beat of his wings tossed Lyn's long hair about, into her face and then back into Greg's.

"Next time I ride in front," he said, laughing, as he tried to brush it off and still hold on. "I can't see anything. Or else you cut your hair!"

"Not on your life! But perhaps Edrina could come with us the next time, and then we could ride separately."

This reminded Greg of a question he had meant to ask.

"Why do you call the Queen 'Dar-mother'?"

"That means there is no blood relationship. She is my father's second wife whom he married only six passings ago. When my sister marries, her husband will be my Dar-brother, and my wife will be her Dar-sister."

"What did Edrina mean when she said she was not yet of age?" Lyn asked.

"At fifty we come of age. She is only forty-eight. I am fifty-nine."

"Fifty!" Lyn exclaimed. "We are almost old by then."

"Fifty is young for us. We are barely full grown by then. According to our laws, no dragon or dragoness may marry before that age without consent of their parents."

"Do they ever elope?" questioned Lyn.

"What does that mean?"

"To run away and get married without the parents' consent."

"And why would a Green Dragon who wears the armband wish to go against the laws when a little waiting would be all that was needed?"

Lyn had no answer for that one, so she changed the subject. "How dreadful of Wondan to pester your sister and to try to make her break your laws."

"That is one of the great problems that have arisen from my father permitting him – on Magior's insistence – to live among us. He is always trying to draw the younger dragons away from our customs and laws which he says are too restrictive."

They were flying over a great forest, whose vast expanse was broken here and there by large meadows, which even from their height looked bright with flowers, and by open spaces where they could see a few dragon homes tucked among the same type of rough lawns and large trees that surrounded the palace.

"Do please fly lower," Lyn begged. He dropped down so that they were then nearly grazing the treetops and the warm air of damp soil and the scents of early summer rose all around them. Once they passed over a grove of some kind of pink and white late-blooming trees and a cloud of fragrance surrounded them for a few moments.

Greg wanted the Prince to drop down to where a river raced through white frothing rapids and then leapt thirty feet down into a quiet, odd-shaped lake. "I've always wanted to try standing behind a waterfall and I think I could do it there; the water arches out as it drops."

"Later I will take you all over the kingdom if you wish," said Damor, "but now I must reach my father before he leaves the Mount." The Mount was a solitary, small mountain that, Damor told them, was in the center of the kingdom lengthwise, but much nearer to the sea than to the border between the Green and Dark Dragon realms. On the side facing the sea was a plateau where the Master of Wisdom and some of the Healers lived. It was from there that Lyn and Greg got their first sight of the

Blue Road, a broad path of brilliant, shimmering blue that was utterly distinct from the blue of the sea and stretched from the shore to the horizon.

Lyn caught her breath and stood still, looking and looking at it. "And that goes Home," she murmured at last in a half whisper without taking her eyes off of it.

"Yes," said Damor.

Greg also stared but only for a moment. The sight made him feel uncomfortable though he did not know why, and he tried to conceal it. "I would like to see it closer. It is probably formed by a current or an odd refraction of light."

"Why do you think it is not really there?" asked a voice behind him. Greg spun around and stood with his mouth open. He knew that the Master of Wisdom was not a green but a purple dragon, but nothing had prepared him for what he saw. He forgot to bow and simply stood staring, as did Lyn. Never had they imagined that any living thing could be so old and yet at the same time look so alive. His body and even his wings were a mass of wrinkles and his purple scales had turned so dark – dragons turn darker with age, not gray – that the original purple showed only here and there. But it was his eyes that held them. There was nothing old about them. On the contrary, they were intensely alive and deep . . . deep and completely still, and somewhere far behind them was a light which Greg later described as a light that shone through all sham and pretense and saw only the truth.

The Master repeated his question. "Why do you think it is not really there?"

Greg tried to look away but could not; the light behind those ancient eyes held him until he said desperately, "It can't be real. How could it be real?"

The Master looked at him and the light in his eyes grew more and more luminous. At last he said, "You will have to find your own answer," and turned to speak with Damor.

CHAPTER 3
Nimeon's Warning

Greg was glad of an excuse to move away. "Damor may want to speak privately to the Master," he said, pulling Lyn by the sleeve.

"Weren't the Master's eyes wonderful?" Lyn said softly as they walked away. "So kind and so wise. The light in them made me think of the Blue Road."

They were passing a group of Dragon-Cousins as she said this.

"You are right. That is where the Master gets so much wisdom, from a lifetime of pondering on the Blue Road. Greetings."

They stopped. The voice sounded familiar but all the Dragon-Cousins looked alike to them.

"Katanga?" Greg asked doubtfully.

"Yes. You do not remember me?"

"You all look so alike," Lyn said apologetically.

The Dragon-Cousin laughed. "Perhaps to you," Katanga replied kindly, "but when you know us you will see how different we are. Look at our backs. No two of us have the same markings. That is how the dragons tell us apart, even in flight."

Along their dull, grayish-green backs, so different from the dragons' brilliant green, were black lines: some wavy, some curved, and some straight, and here and there was a black blotch or two. Katanga had three distinct lines that started from a broad patch on his head and gradually faded until only the center one went the full length of his tail.

"Simpler than fingerprints," Greg commented to his sister.

"Next time we'll recognize you at once," said Lyn, afraid that his feelings might have been hurt. She added in surprise, "How did you get here? It is so far." She could not imagine a Dragon-Cousin being able to cover that distance overnight.

Katanga chuckled. "A dragon friend carried me. I am learning to be a Healer, and came here to consult those whose knowledge is far greater than mine."

"So that is why you were asked to take care of the child's cut foot yesterday. Is he going to be all right?" Greg asked.

Katanga chuckled again. "It was only a bad cut, and the mother knew it. If the wound had been more serious she would have called on Orimalgon, who is one of the best Healers in the kingdom."

Greg looked back over his shoulder to where Damor and the Master were talking. "Did we come in time? Is the King still here?"

"There is the King," Katanga motioned with his head. On the far side of the plateau facing the sea lay the King. His eyes were closed and he lay without stirring. "At last he realizes – for I heard him say so – that the evil foretold by Nimeon the Great has come upon us and for much of what is wrong he is to blame because he failed to rule as the King of the Green Dragons should."

"What do you mean by 'the evil foretold by Nimeon the Great'?" said Lyn.

44

Katanga settled himself comfortably and the twins sat down beside him. "When Nimeon the Great bade farewell to his people before fighting the Great Sea Serpent, he said what every child since then has had to learn:

'Farewell, O my beloved people. Serve my son as you have served me, and above all, serve the Great One and be faithful to His laws. Then the realm of the Green Dragons will ever prosper. But if you depart from His laws, the peace of the land will be shattered and the darkness of strife will fall. Farewell, my beloved son: be a wise and just King and more than all the others serve the Great One. Farewell.'

"Nimeon was followed by his son, Filaron, who was a good and able King, though not a great one, and so was his son. After them came a decline. Our present King's father was weak and indifferent, careless of the laws of the Great One, and paid no attention to the warnings of the Master. Had not his reign been short, as it was, many evils would have come.

"In this our King is not like his father. He has never gone against the laws of the Great One, but he has done little to see that they were upheld by all. In his youth he was a great warrior. Fighting has been his sole interest. As long as his first Queen lived, Damor's and Edrina's mother, he listened to her for he loved her and often let himself be guided by her wisdom. It was she who supervised the training of Damor and Edrina. But alas, soon after she went

Home, some ten passings ago, he was severely injured in a great battle and has been partly crippled and in pain ever since. So now he spends his time dreaming of his past exploits and grows more bitter as his suffering increases.

"Magior, who had long been the King's friend, though the Queen mistrusted him, was then able to install himself in the King's closest circle. It was he who urged the King to remarry and persuaded him to ask for his sister. He then told his sister, who is much younger than himself, that it was her duty to marry the crippled King, though it is said she loved another dragon. Poor Queen, I fear she is not happy. Indeed, I think they both regret their marriage."

"What is the Queen like? Is she also an intriguer? She seems very different from her brother," Lyn asked, thinking of the Queen's nervous fussiness.

"I know no evil of the Queen. Weak she may be, but she comes faithfully to the Master, and since her frail little son was born last summer, she has brought him here many times, hoping the Healers could give him strength. She stays here with him and talks often with the Master. Once I saw her weeping as she spoke. I fear the only happiness she has left is her child, and I doubt she will have him much longer as he is so sickly. Last winter he nearly went Home because his chest is so weak and he caught a cold which is often fatal to the very young dragons, but the Master managed to save him."

"Why is it so important for the dragons to come here frequently?" demanded Greg, looking over to where the King still lay facing the sea.

"All dragons and Dragon-Cousins should come

here at least twice a year to speak with the Master, spending time looking at the Blue Road and being refreshed in thought."

"Do you all think the same thing?" asked Greg.

"No, the Master helps each to know what his life needs. But alas, when the King fails to come, others follow his example, a few at first and then more. Fortunately the Captain of the Border Guard is one of the most faithful and insists that the warriors come, so they are better trained than many others. This is good, for they are the ones who have most contact with the Dark Dragons, who have nothing but contempt for the Master and the Blue Road, as I told you. The young, too, are still sent. Their mothers see to that. Over there the Young Master is teaching those children who are here for the first time."

Under a nearby tree was another purple dragon who was speaking to a little group of small dragons and dragonesses. The Young Master, for that is what the Master's assistant is called, was not old, but in his prime, as his scales were a rich purple and gleamed like the most expensive amethysts. He finished speaking and the little group bowed their heads respectfully. He led them to the edge of the plateau and lined them up looking towards the sea and the Blue Road, the four dragons a little apart from the three dragonesses.

"What are they doing?"

"Learning to think over what he has taught them."

The little dragons lay quietly for a surprising length of time (in human terms), then one small dragon began to twitch his tail, a little at first, then more and more, until he found he could just touch the companion on each side of him. They at once twitched back, and so did the fourth until with high-pitched squeals they pounced on each other in a glorious roughhouse. The little dragonesses, tempted beyond endurance, scurried over and joined in the fun by tweaking the various tails that were waving wildly about. The Young Master came over and quietly restored order with a gentle reprimand and lined them up again, but this time far apart. Shortly afterwards he sent them off to have a romp with one of the dragonesses who helped care for the sick.

"Why do you call him the 'Young Master'? He doesn't look very young to me," said Greg.

"No, he is not young; he is a hundred and twelve passings, but that is the custom. He will be the next Master, and when there is one younger, as there should be, he would be the Very Young Master."

Katanga sounded sad and Lyn asked him why.

"It is a great sorrow and anxiety to all of us that there is no Very Young Master. Never in all the history of the Green Dragons has there been such a length of time between the birth of one Master and the next. One hundred and twelve passings and no new Master," he repeated half to himself.

Greg thought this would be a good moment to point out that since they believed in signs, this might be a sign that a Master was no longer needed and the time had come for the dragons to each do and think as they pleased. "Perhaps the time has come for you to be more scientific," he began. He stopped. Even to him the words sounded hollow. It must be this place, he told himself. Well, he would explain it to Katanga and Damor when they were back at the palace.

"Who are the parents of a Master?" Lyn asked.

"Any couple may be. No one knows when or to whom a Master will be born. Even if the parents have other children, they do not think the egg is different until a new little Master comes forth."

Damor had been talking with his father and now came over to them.

"I must leave you for a time as I have to take a message from my father to a former member of the Council in whom my father, and my mother also, had great confidence."

"Please let us come with you," cried Greg. "It's such fun riding on your back."

The Prince hesitated for a moment. "Very well. It is not far."

Once again, this time with Greg in front, they were up and climbing higher and higher. Damor flew faster this time, so much so that Lyn became frightened, and fearing she could not hold on against such a rush of wind, begged him to go slower. He did, but soon started to circle down, saying, "If you do not mind, I am going to leave you here in this open place just below that group of houses. I cannot fly fast enough with you on my back and it is urgent that I return to my father as soon as I can. There is no danger. The two you need to fear are at the palace. Do not worry. I shall be back shortly."

Neither Greg nor Lyn like the idea of being left

alone in a strange forest, but had to say yes. They watched him shoot up into the air and, gathering speed, he was out of sight in a moment.

They looked around. It was a lovely spot.

"Damor wouldn't have left us here if he hadn't known we would be perfectly safe. Let's explore a bit," said Greg. "I hear water running over there. I want a drink."

"Yes, flying makes me thirsty. Here is a path. It must be for dragons because it's so wide. Let's follow it. We can't get lost that way. We musn't go far or else we won't hear Damor when he comes back."

In a moment the path curved and ran alongside a wide, shallow brook that was tumbling noisily over stones and bubbling into quiet pools. On the other side, just a little way up the slope, was a dragon house and right in front of it was a dragoness who was filling a container at the stream. She was old and wrinkled and, this surprised them, thin and wretched looking. She looked up and peered at them.

"Who are you? I do not see well anymore."

"We are children from a place called Earth. Your King gave us leave to visit and Prince Damor brought us here. He will be back directly," Lyn answered hurriedly, though the dragoness looked so sad and old that she did not fear her.

"Ah," was all the dragoness replied and began slowly and with great difficulty to climb the short slope.

"Here, let us help you," said Lyn jumping across the brook by means of two flat stones. She and Greg carried the container between them to the house where an even older and equally wretched dragon was lying. He looked ill.

"Thank you," said the dragoness. "My husband has a fever and neither of us have eaten for days."

Greg and Lyn looked at each other. They found it hard to believe that there was such wretchedness and neglect in the land of the Green Dragons.

"Couldn't the Healers help you?" asked Greg. "Or don't they make house calls?" He had thought the Healers would be like his uncle who went wherever he was needed at any hour of the day or night.

"I am sure they could. But no one comes near us now. I did ask the young couple up there to go for them, as it is too far for me; but they never went. Things have changed since the Dark Dragons came to live here."

"Came to live here!" exclaimed Lyn. "I thought only Wondan was allowed to live in this kingdom."

"A pair of young Dark ones – though I doubt if they are married – settled in an empty house over there not long ago. One of the families already here would not live near them because they ridiculed some of our laws, so that family left. There is another couple, who used to look in on us every day, but now pay little attention to us. This land is not what it once was," she ended with a sigh.

"We'll tell Prince Damor. I'm sure he will help you right away," Lyn said sympathetically, while Greg poured water from the container into a bowl and placed it in front of the old dragon. They carried up several more containers of water so the dragons would have a handy supply. Then the sound of wings was heard overhead.

"Damor!" Greg cried and tore down the path, leaving Lyn with the old couple.

When the Prince landed, Greg told him breathlessly what they had found. At first, Damor was totally unbelieving and positively snorted, "An old couple neglected in this land? Impossible!"

He followed Greg and his disbelief turned to anger at the sight. "That this should happen among the Green Dragons!" He was shooting out flame. "But what do you mean about a Dark couple living here? I know my father never gave such a permission. He shall have to hear about this at once." Damor hurried along another path with the twins trotting along behind him.

At the top of the slope were three other houses placed well apart – the dragons like privacy. In front of one of them were two dragonesses, one Green and one Dark, talking together.

Ignoring the Dark one, Damor spoke to the Green Dragoness. Indignantly he reproached her for leaving the old couple hungry and in need of help. "Were you too lazy to at least do them the kindness of flying the short distance to the Mount and telling the Healers?"

She started and looked ashamed. "We did . . . I used to . . . or rather the other couple who lived here took care of them, and when they left, this one," with a wave of her head towards the Dark Dragoness, "said she would," she answered with considerable confusion. "Perhaps I should have gone anyway . . ." Her voice trailed off.

The Prince turned on the Dark Dragoness. "Who gave you permission to live here?"

"The Prime Minister, Magior. And why should we not live here?" she answered with a note of insolence in her voice.

"Prime Minister!" snorted Damor. "There is no such person. Only the King can give such a permission – and I am certain he did not."

She tossed her head and without replying turned her back on the Prince and went into the house.

"Lady," the Prince said earnestly to the Green Dragoness, "in neglecting this old couple, you have forgotten the promises you made when you received the armband. Now I charge you to let nothing happen to them until the Healers can bring them to the Mount."

The dragoness gave a slow nod.

"Get on my back," Damor said abruptly to Greg and Lyn. Breathing out fire and smoke heats up a dragon's whole body. The Prince was so hot, the children could barely stand it. He flew carefully, but smoke poured from his nostrils and streamed back into Greg's face and made him cough so hard he was afraid he would shake loose. Lyn fared better as she hid her face against Greg's back and escaped with only stinging eyes.

At the Mount, Damor explained the situation to the Young Master. He was just as indignant as the Prince and said he would go there at once and bring the sick couple to the Mount.

The King was speaking with the Master and the Captain of the Border Guard who had arrived in the meantime. He was a tough, powerful dragon, who wore, besides the gold band on his right arm, a broad bronze one on his left, the mark of his office.

Damor repeated the story to his father. Damor had been angry but it was nothing compared to the King's fury.

"Neglected . . . wretched . . . starving in my kingdom! Help must be taken them at once! And a Dark couple living here without my permission? I shall drive them out myself!" he roared, shooting out such enormous flames that though Greg was several feet from him, he jumped back to escape their heat.

"Father, the Young Master left at once when I told him," Damor said. "He is bringing them here. As to the Dark pair, I suspect there may be others whom Magior has invited to live here without your permission. Would it not be best to find out how many there are before they can warn each other and perhaps hide? The Captain can bring this pair here to you and then keep them under guard until all are found and sent over the border together."

The King calmed down a little. "That is good advice, my son. Bring them and the negligent Green Dragons here to justice," he commanded the Captain. The Captain flew off and the King remained where he was, his eyes glowing with anger.

"How will the old dragons get here?" Lyn asked. "I don't think they are strong enough to fly."

"They must have some means of carrying the sick and wounded," Greg said, though he wondered himself.

Damor overheard them. "They will be carried in nets made of vines." He looked in the direction in which lay the houses. "There, look: one is already in the air."

Not having a dragon's keen sight, the children

could see nothing at that distance except a big black spot. Before long, though, they were able to make out two dragons with a large net slung between them. In it was the sick dragon. He was placed gently near one of the buildings and then the dragons flew off for the dragoness. Soon she was safely set down. Shortly after, the Captain accompanied by two warriors arrived with the Dark and Green couples.

"These," said the Captain motioning to the Green Dragons, "came at once upon hearing your order, Sire, but these Dark villains refused until forced to."

"Well," said the King sitting upright. "What have you to say, you who wear the gold armband and yet neglected the elderly and weak until they would have starved, had these Children from Earth not found them?"

The Green Dragoness was weeping. "You are right, Your Majesty," she acknowledged. "I let myself listen too easily to one who promised to do what I should have done," here she looked up, "but do not blame my husband, the fault was far more mine. He is often away on his duties."

"No, it was mine, too," said her husband gruffly. "I knew they were there and that the old need the comfort of visits as do my own parents."

"And what have you Dark ones to say?" asked the King. "You say you were given permission to live here. I gave no such permission. Nor may any remain here without learning our ways. Have they ever come here to you, Master?"

The Master shook his head. "Never."

"Then," said the King, "since you have shown no desire to learn our ways, you must depart at once."

The Dark couple had been listening with a nonchalant attitude. Evidently they had made up their minds that they were going to be expelled and were going to have their say.

"Well, of course, we are sorry if the lives of that worn out pair are important to you," the dragon retorted sarcastically, "but why bother about them? We Dark Dragons never do. The old are useless, just a burden. And if what you call . . . um . . . the Blue Road . . . is so wonderful, and you believe in it, why not just help them get along it faster?"

The other couple stared at their erstwhile friends as though suddenly seeing them in a new and unpleasant light, and the dragoness gasped with horror.

The King roared in fury and lashed his tail. "Keep them carefully under guard, Captain, while you search out every Dark Dragon in the land. Then take them all to the border, and never permit any of them to cross it again."

During this time Greg noticed that while the young Green couple sat where they had happened to land, facing the Blue Road, the Dark couple did not once look at it and deliberately placed themselves so their backs were towards it. He had the feeling that for the dragons there was no half way: they either had to accept or deny its existence. He wondered uneasily if this applied to humans as well.

After the Captain and his warriors flew off with the Dark pair, the King said to the Master, "By tomorrow night the kingdom will be swept clean of them."

The Master looked at the Blue Road, then said quietly, "Of their presence, but what of their ideas? How much have they taken root, especially in the minds of the young?"

The King was silent for a long time. When he spoke, his tone was deeper and quieter and he sounded weary and sad. "The fault is mine. All look to the King for guidance, which I have failed to give. I will do my best to undo the harm which has been done." He was again silent, then he lifted his head and said as though he were looking far away, "But will time be given me?"

"I do not know," said the Master, and the light behind his eyes was barely gleaming.

Later Greg, who was wandering around, heard the two Green Dragons apologizing to the elderly couple. "Come back as soon as you feel better and live in the house next to us. Truly you will be as grandparents to us."

Greatly relieved, Greg ran to tell Damor. "If all the Green Dragons react that way, everything will be all right again quickly."

Damor did not answer and Greg wondered why.

Later the Queen flew in with a carrying basket which she took at once to the Master. The Princess was with her.

"She fears her little son is ill again," Edrina explained. The Queen remained a long time with the Master and when she left him she was noticeably less nervous and fussy.

In the meantime, Lyn had found a friend in the

Young Master. Katanga had brought her over to him, and the three sat looking at the Blue Road and talking as though they had known each other for years. "There is not the same air about him as with the Master, and yet, he too is wise and kind," she confided later to Katanga.

"There is only one true Master and he has special powers. It is the same with the King. Special powers come with the kingship."

Lyn wanted very much to speak with the Master but felt he might think it presuming of her. As though he guessed her thoughts he came over to her.

"What troubles you, Child from Earth?" he asked. As she looked into his eyes she forgot all fear, all everything, until he repeated gently, "What troubles you, Child from Earth?"

"My brother." She knew she did not have to explain. The Master would understand.

"Let him look upon the Blue Road. Only truth is seen there."

A short time later the royal family flew back to the palace together with Greg on Damor's back and Lyn on Edrina's. The King was less gruff and so Greg took courage and said, "We are very glad if our coming has in any way helped you, but we still don't know why we are here, if, as you said, there must be a reason."

"You will find the reason if you are willing to," said the King.

"But truly we are very happy to be here," Lyn threw in quickly. She already loved the dragons and their land. "I do hope Your Majesty will allow us to

58

stay here at least for a while."

"You may remain until you must go," was his strange answer.

When they passed between the saluting guard, the King ordered two of them to the ground and told them to wait.

Magior and Wondan were on the terrace, and as soon as the party was down, Magior began to inquire after the King's health with the deepest of bows, which became a positive undulation of the head.

"Like a serpent," Lyn said in a whisper to Greg. She was beside Damor who overheard her.

"Only too true," was his equally low comment.

The King made an impatient movement. Magior at once stopped his bows and said in a tone of greatest affection, "I have been so anxious about you, Sire, and would that others had shared my anxiety," he began, with a meaningful glance at the Prince. "Is there any duty or task I can perform to relieve you of the many burdens of your kingship?"

"Be silent," said the King sternly. Magior started in surprise. "Or rather, answer: how did you dare to tell certain Dark Dragons they might dwell in this kingdom?"

Magior was taken back for a moment, then bowed more obsequiously and said in a voice smoother than ever, "Forgive me, Sire, if I erred, but you are often ill, and since you gave permission for Wondan to live here at the palace . . . and this was such a nice couple, I thought it would be in your mind to let them stay. Of course, I expected them to come at once and speak with you, Sire, but they probably feared to disturb you as I told them your health was not what it once was. And I knew that the Queen, my sister," (there was a slight emphasis on the last word as though to remind the King of their relationship) "was too worried about the little Prince to wish a visit from the dragonesses . . ." His voice trailed off in the face of the King's anger.

"What else have you done without my knowledge?" continued the King without taking his eyes off Magior. "Much, I fear." The King's whole manner had changed. He no longer roared but spoke in a tone of cold, hard, purposeful determination, which was far more terrifying.

"Depart from here and find yourself another place to live, or go to the Dark ones since you have grown so friendly with them. But if you do, then never return to this kingdom."

Magior started to protest, but the King silenced him and swung towards Wondan.

"To you on an evil day I did give permission to remain here for a while, but your stay has lengthened far beyond my intention."

Wondan gave a quick glance at Magior. "Sire," he answered almost as smoothly as Magior, "if I have overstayed your permission, it was because of my love for you and your family, especially your charming daughter. Now I ask to remain hoping that in some way I shall win her favor."

"I have told you that I would never accept the proposal of anyone who does not love the Great One and obey His laws," answered the Princess in a firm and dignified manner.

"You have my daughter's answer, an answer of which I am proud," said the King. "Now this is mine: when you asked to remain here for a visit I gave you leave only on the condition that you would go to the Master and strive to learn the laws of the Great One. You agreed, but the Master says you have never been to the Mount or looked on the Blue Road."

"Well, perhaps I have been negligent in that matter. But surely there is no need to go any more to the Master, for since none have been born within the usual time, that must be a sign that soon there will be none. Then you, like us, will find you do not need a Master."

Greg was startled. Wondan's thoughts were so like his.

The King ignored Wondan's speech and said more coldly than ever, "I gave you my conditions. You have not obeyed them. Instead I heard you have been trying to draw some of our young to the ways of the Dark Dragons."

Wondan did not deny this. He merely gave an evil chuckle, stared back at the King, and said threateningly, "Perhaps Your Majesty would do well to remember that I am a close friend of our King and that he is a great warrior." This was said with a contemptuous glance towards the King's crippled wing. "Any day, unless otherwise advised, he might decide to extend his kingdom . . . and the Green Dragons are no longer the great warriors they once were, or . . ." (with another evil chuckle) "thought they were."

Damor, his eyes flaming and smoke pouring

from his nostrils, flung himself forward. The Princess was also smoking. Greg grabbed Lyn and pulled her back to the shelter of the doorway, certain that flames would be shooting forth all around in a moment.

The King alone did not move and motioned Damor back.

"Father," cried the Prince furiously, "after such an insult, let me engage him in combat!"

"No, my son," said the King in a tone so hard and cold that Lyn shivered. "He came as my guest, and unless he is the aggressor, I would not have him slain here in my palace." He called the two waiting guards to come forward. "Drive this Wondan from our land. Then let it be known all along the border that if he ever tries to cross it again, he is to be engaged in combat at once and either slain or driven back."

When Wondan began to hurl further threats, the guards who had also heard the insulting speech knocked him into the air. This they did by whacking his soft undersides with their hard heads, and when he failed to move fast enough to suit them, they added a short breath of flame which forced him to leap upwards, flailing at them in return and roaring threats.

The King watched them out of sight and then turned to Magior.

"Go," he commanded. Magior spread his wings, then closed them.

"I go first to say farewell to my sister, since I am driven from her by her husband and my Darbrother," he said, and went into the palace before the King could reply.

The King paid no attention to him. He gave a long, deep sigh. "Stay with me, my son and daughter," he said, and again sounded weary and sad. He then remained silent with his eyes closed for a long time.

"What shall we do?" Greg whispered to Edrina who was nearest him.

"Stay close to us," she whispered back, "until we know what is going to happen."

CHAPTER 4
Treachery in the Night

The rest of the day dragged by slowly. The King remained in the same place, silent and still, only twitching his crippled side occasionally. Damor never left him, and the twins were chatting in low tones with him. Edrina, at Damor's whispered suggestion, had gone to the Queen hoping to find out something about Magior's plans, when a warrior brought to the King a Green Dragon couple and a half-grown Dark Dragoness.

"Sire," said the warrior. "When she was ordered to leave the land, this youngster begged so earnestly to be brought to you that I have done so."

"Sire," pleaded the young dragoness, and from the way she turned her head, they could see she was blind in her left eye, "please let me remain. I will gladly do whatever is required of me if only I may stay here."

"She has been as a daughter to us, ever since she came," said the other dragoness, "and we would adopt her."

"How old are you?" inquired the King. "And why did you leave your own land to come here?"

"I am twenty-eight, Sire," said the dragoness. "Ten passings ago I lost my eye in an accident, and ever since I have been made fun of by the other children and grown dragons, too, and pushed aside as useless until I was miserable. I heard the Green Dragons were kind to the injured and that they sometimes adopted the young of our land and brought them up as their own children.

"So one night I slipped across the Border and, after living hidden in your land a short time, saw the lady Morna gathering rushes. As she seemed to be having difficulty," ("Rheumatism," murmured the older dragoness.) "I helped her and have been doing so ever since. They have been like a mother and father to me. Please let me stay. I cannot bear to go back." She began to weep.

"Have you been to learn from the Master?" the King asked sternly.

The young dragoness looked piteously at the elderly couple.

"No," said the dragon, "and the fault is ours, not hers. Ever since she came to us she has asked to be taught the laws of the Great One and has begged us over and over again to take her to the Master that she might learn more. We go twice a year and have put her off, saying we would take her next time we went."

"She, the stranger, asked to be taken to the Master and you, the Green Dragons, would not." The King's statement rang out like an accusation. Both of the Green Dragons dropped their heads and nodded sorrowfully.

"I hope your father will let her stay," Lyn murmured to Damor.

"Be still," was his answer.

The King's next words were in a more gentle tone. "How did you hear of our ways, child?"

"Where I lived there were Dragon-Cousins who had been captured and forced to work. They were kind to me when I was in pain, and told me how different were the ways of the Green Dragons and that I might hope to be adopted if I came here."

"How many are held captive in that place?"

"Four, and two children. Please may I stay?"

After a long silence the King said almost kindly, "It is better that you go back to your own. The day may soon come when no Dark Dragon is welcome here."

"I will gladly risk that," replied the young dragoness.

When the King shook his head she came closer to him, leaned forward and said something which the twins could not hear. He called Damor over and they all spoke together in low tones and seemed to be discussing something earnestly. Then the group flew away, Damor with them. Later when he came back, Lyn asked him what had happened to the little dragoness.

"She was sent over the border, weeping and indignant," was his answer.

"What a shame!" cried Lyn. "Couldn't your father have allowed one little dragoness to stay? She wouldn't have hurt you and she was so pathetic."

"And she wanted so much to go to the Master!" Greg exclaimed in surprise. He had thought that would surely have won her the right to stay and found himself wishing it had.

The next morning Damor had an errand with the head of the Fisher Dragons, those dragons who live by the sea and do all the fishing for both the dragons and Dragon-Cousins.

"Please let us go with you, if you are not in a hurry," Greg begged. "Since we are not allowed to wander around and explore, there is nothing for us to do. When you are away we have to stay close to Edrina and she has to be with the Queen."

"Certainly," answered Damor, "I am in no hurry today."

It was a perfect summer morning. Even in flight the sun was warm and there was only the slightest of breezes. Every now and then they met a dragon or dragon family who were taking their "morning flight", as the dragons say. Once as they passed over a group of houses, a dragon couple flew up with their two children who were excited at seeing two strange creatures and flew around the Prince asking questions. One was so curious that he swooped too close and nearly knocked Greg off.

"Stop that!" Greg yelled.

The father darted over and forcibly removed his mischievous youngster by the simple expedient of grabbing his tail and pulling him backwards, then spanked him twice with his head while apologizing to Damor and Greg.

"Are you all right, Greg?" Damor asked.

"Yes, but we both nearly went off!"

The sea was calm, barely moving in long, slow swells. When Greg saw the flat, hard, wet sand, he shouted, "What a perfect place to practice sprinting!" and jumped off Damor's back as they landed. He ran down to near the water's edge, poised himself, and shot forward.

Several fisher dragons were lying around.

"Another day without fishing, we fear," they had called back in answer to Damor's greeting. Now they watched Greg with interest. "Is that the way you race?" one asked. "We also race, but in the air."

"Yes," Greg said. Then he had an idea. "Do you start your races in the air or from the ground?"

"Sometimes one way, sometimes another," replied the dragon.

"Look, I'll race you, but you must start from the ground and I must be the one to mark the course."

The dragons agreed enthusiastically. Greg marked a length he hoped would be less than the dragons would require to reach their full speed from a ground position, but one in which he knew he could. "You be the starter," he told Lyn.

The beach was broad and there was plenty of room for two dragons to be a wingspread apart with Greg in the middle. Lyn took off a brightly colored scarf she was wearing and stood at the water's edge.

"When she says 'Go' and waves the scarf, that's the blue and white thing in her hand, we start," Greg explained.

"On your mark . . . Get set . . . Go!" Lyn shouted at the top of her voice and waved the scarf vigorously.

The dragons flung themselves upward and forwards. Greg shot out ahead of them and easily reached the marker before they had gotten into their full wingbeat.

They at once wanted to try again. This time they were closer behind him and by the fourth attempt they were nearly up with him. He was tiring while the dragons were barely warming up.

He rested a while and then was ready to try again. They lined up, but this time Lyn, as the tide was rising, unthinkingly moved closer to the nearest dragon. As she waved her scarf and he leapt into flight, he caught her with his wing and flipped her upwards in such a way that she turned a complete somersault and landed in the sea. She hit the sandy bottom hard and it took her a moment to realize which way was up. She came to the surface unharmed, but coughing and sputtering. The water was only up to her chest, and she waved the scarf she was still clutching to a dragon who was hovering overhead, to show that she was all right. In an instant she was caught up and before she could catch her breath, was deposited gently on the beach.

"I'm all right," she said between coughs to the anxious group around her. "I'm not a bit hurt."

"You should have seen how fast he took off. You were still flipping in the air," Greg told her.

From the way the dragons were complimenting her rescuer, she realized they had thought she was drowning, and pulled herself together enough to thank him as though he had saved her.

"That is the way we rescue any member of our fishing teams, if he gets caught in a line or net and dragged into the water," her rescuer explained.

"We can't swim," a dragoness remarked, "but it seems to me that the old tales say the Earth people could."

"Yes, we do," Lyn answered. "I love to swim."

"How do you do it? Like a fish?"

"No, indeed," Lyn said laughing. "I'll show you how. I couldn't be wetter than I am."

She had been a little envious of the dragons' admiration of Greg's racing ability and was glad of the opportunity to be the center of attention. She took off her shoes and waded out, then swam around while the dragons circled above, watching her performance and applauding her. Pleased with herself, she swam out a short distance farther, then came back. She was in waist-deep water wading towards the shore when she felt something curl itself around her ankle.

A vivid picture of a huge and evil-looking brute she had seen in an aquarium flashed across her mind.

"Octopus!" she yelled, panic-stricken, and plunged forward, certain as it made a second curl around her leg that she would be pulled into the sea and drowned before she could reach the shore. Greg dashed toward the water but before he could reach her, she was splashing onto the safety of the beach. She looked down. A large, fat eel was uncurling itself from her ankle.

"Ugh!" she cried, and kicked it off. As it slid back towards the sea, a dragoness caught it and snapped its head off, then dropped it onto the sand where it continued to wriggle.

"What a clever way to catch eels," the dragoness remarked. "Could you please catch one for me? They are delicious and yet hard to catch as they generally slip through our nets."

"You can have this one," Lyn said with a shudder. "I don't want it. And we don't catch eels that way." She flatly refused to try again.

The dragons were ready for another race. Greg,

however, wasn't. He was glad that Damor wanted to leave, as he did not think he could win again.

Back at the palace, Lyn sat in the sun to dry. She emptied her pockets and was pleased to find her purse had not been lost during her dunking and resolved in the future to keep it with her jacket which was in Edrina's room. Greg flopped down beside her and closed his eyes. He was dozing when Lyn poked him awake.

"Look! Look!"

The elderly couple of the previous day and the young Dark Dragoness, whose wings were drooping from exhaustion, had dropped down accompanied this time by no less than the Captain of the Border Guard himself.

"Sire," said the Captain, "this child did as she promised and led the four captive Dragon-Cousins to where we could take them to safety while she carried the two young ones herself, though their weight was really too much for her strength."

"Please may I stay now?" begged the little dragoness.

The King leaned over and touched her on the head. "I thank you, brave child, in the name of all our Dragon-Cousins. Go with your new parents and be a loving daughter to them.

"And you, her parents, take good care of your new daughter and teach her well our ways."

"We go from here straight to the Master," answered the dragon, while the little dragoness joyfully wept her thanks. As they flew off, the King ordered the Captain to go with them and to tell the Master the tale of her bravery.

"Damor, what did you mean by saying she wept and was indignant when pushed over the border?" Lyn demanded accusingly.

Damor chuckled. "She played her part well, and none suspected what she was planning to do."

During the next few days the change in the King became more and more evident. Instead of spending only a short time each morning on the terrace, he lay there all day and patiently listened to all who came to him and encouraged each one.

On the third day, Damor told the twins that although the border was now being closely watched, even the most experienced warriors could report no sign of an impending attack.

"Do you think Wondan's threats were empty ones?" Greg asked.

"It is too soon to tell," was Damor's reply.

The twins hoped everything was settling down. Though they were now allowed more freedom and could wander around the palace and palace grounds, what they wanted to do was fly. Damor promised them that after this crisis was over he would take them all over the kingdom, and they could not wait.

That afternoon the whole royal family was on the lawn enjoying the sun – even the King was in an unusually pleasant mood – when a messenger dragon hurtled through the sky and dropped at a terrific speed.

"Sire, my news is terrible. The Young Master was called out on an errand of healing, a ruse no doubt, and was attacked by two Dark warriors. They would have slain him except for some of our warriors who saw the attack. One Dark Dragon they slew, but the other escaped, and they thought it was Wondan. The Young Master was carried at once to the Mount, but those who bore him said he was dying."

The dragons were stunned, and dragons are not easily stunned. No one, not even the Queen, moved or spoke for a long time.

At length the Princess cried out, weeping, "My father, my father, what has brought this calamity upon us?" and then the Queen burst into loud wails.

Damor said, as though torn with mental agony, "And there is no Very Young Master. Even if one were born today, the Master is too old to live until he were grown. What is going to happen to us?"

The King said nothing. His eyes had darkened as though the life had gone out of them. He, Lyn guessed, understood best of all of them the full import of this tragedy.

At last he stirred and said, "Damor, come with me," and flew off.

The rest of the day passed miserably. Even the Queen did not fuss over her son, a sad, thin little baby of one passing who crawled around feebly on the sunny lawn. Its green scales were dull, and it had no markings to speak of, but that is not unusual with baby dragons. On many, the markings do not become definite until the second or third passing.

The atmosphere was one of anxious waiting, and Greg and Lyn, feeling in the way, sat by themselves under a tree or wandered aimlessly around. Towards sunset they heard a group of Dragon-Cousins in the courtyard murmuring sorrowfully. "The

Young Master has gone Home," they were told, "a dragon told us so."

Feeling more in the way than ever, and sad for the dragons' sake, they went to the terrace where the Queen and Edrina were weeping at the news. They soon went into the palace. Lyn was also crying at the loss of her new friend. Greg felt like doing the same and to stop himself became disagreeable. "It's too bad they feel that way, but as I was going to say on the Mount, only . . . um . . . it didn't seem the right place . . . perhaps it's the best thing for them. They will have to learn not to be so dependent. They will have to become more scientific."

"Stop it!" Lyn shouted at him. "You're like the Dark Dragons. Go back through the Door. You don't belong here." She ran crying into the palace. Greg remained on the terrace, angry and ashamed of himself for having been nasty to his sister, as he was generally a kind boy. He also began to wonder if perhaps she was right and he did not belong in this extraordinary land, and was surprised at how miserable the thought made him. He didn't like being left alone and followed her slowly into the palace. When he found her she had her arms around Edrina's neck and they were comforting each other. He again felt he didn't belong and heaved himself silently onto a chest. Lyn never bore resentments, and as soon as she saw him she came over and climbed up beside him. He put his arm around her and gave her a hug, and she understood he was sorry.

The following morning when the King and Damor returned, the Queen greeted them with a wail of sorrow. "We have heard the evil news that

74

the Young Master has gone Home. What shall we do now? Alas! Alas!" she wept.

The King gave her a sharp look and silenced Damor who was about to speak; then, without answering her, he went into the palace followed by Damor and the still-lamenting Queen.

The atmosphere was so sorrowful and gloomy that Lyn asked Damor if they should go back to Earth. "We may have helped your father, though I wonder if he thinks so now. Does he blame us for all this? It is as though we were the small stones that started an avalanche."

"He blames no one except himself," Damor assured her. "No, your coming was more like a spark which lit the fire that showed us where we have failed. Do not go. Your presence gives me hope."

In the early twilight, they stopped in the kitchen to ask the friendly cook for a snack and choked over the strong, bitter odor coming from a pot simmering over the open fire. The cook explained that it was a special potion that Orimalgon was brewing for the King to help deaden his pain. She gave them chunks from a hot loaf she had just taken from the oven and some fruit, and after thanking her, the children hurried out into the courtyard where they could breathe again. They settled down in an out-of-the-way corner. Lyn was about to take a bite when she gasped, "Magior!"

Greg looked up quickly. "Where? I don't see him."

"I thought I saw him in the storeroom where we were that first day. He peered around the edge of the doorway and looked as though he hated the sight of us. Do you think we should tell Damor?"

"I don't think he would dare come here, not after the way the King sent him off. Is Magior there?" he called to a Dragon-Cousin who was coming out of the storeroom with a basket perched on his back. "My sister thinks she saw him."

"Magior? No, indeed! He's not going to trouble us again. We've had too much of him," was the sharp answer. The Dragon-Cousin left his basket by the kitchen door and came over and chatted with them about the kitchen work while they ate. "Tomorrow is one of our baking days," he said. "Come early and I will show you how the ovens work. Perhaps your sister would also want to see it."

Greg accepted the offer enthusiastically, and Lyn added her polite thanks. She was still uneasy about Magior, however, and was relieved when the Queen came looking for Orimalgon and asked them to come in. "The King is in such pain tonight . . . no wonder, after all the terrible things that have happened . . . and perhaps Orimalgon will want you to try to distract him while he rubs His Majesty's bad wing. Just stay here, please. I know you won't mind waiting, my dears. I am sorry to leave you alone, but I always remain in the room next to the King's in case he should want me. Also, there I can keep an eye on our little son who is right across the way. The poor baby is coughing again and I am *so* worried about him. I would take him to the Master, but the night is unusually chilly and I do not want to leave the King. Oh dear, so many troubles come at once . . ." and off she went.

"I'm glad she's gone," said Greg with a sigh of

relief.

"I feel sorry for her," said Lyn, thoughtfully. "After what Katanga told us, I can't help feeling that she keeps fussing around so as to forget how unhappy she is."

Once before, Orimalgon had brought them to distract the King while he rubbed his aching wing and leg with an orange-colored ointment that had a strong but pleasant odor. Spicy, Lyn described it, but not like any spices of Earth. The King had been in a dark and morose mood that time and at first had only been gruffly polite to them. Orimalgon, however, had been so skillful in his questioning them about Earth that the King had gradually become interested and asked questions himself – strong, pointed questions that had left Greg wondering if some of the things he admired on Earth were really worth admiring.

They waited and waited. Dinnertime came and still they had not been called. The Queen had not forgotten them, however, and dinner was brought to them. Damor joined them – the Queen had begged Edrina to stay with her – and was far less sorrowful than the twins had expected. Edrina soon came, and they chatted like old friends.

It was very late when the Queen came and told them to go to bed. The King would not need them this night, as Orimalgon was going to give him the special potion that would dull the pain and let him rest.

Lyn was so sleepy she could barely keep her eyes open as she followed the Princess to her room, and Greg once stumbled over the Prince's tail. He remembered Damor's remark about warrior's tails and woke up enough to apologize. Damor just chuckled. Greg tumbled into his bed and was asleep before Damor had time to curl up on his.

Greg's dreams were wild. He was constantly running away from dragons and dogs who turned into dragons and came after him in full cry. He woke up with their cries ringing in his ears. Then he realized the cries were real and in the moonlight saw Damor hurrying out of the room. He jumped up and ran over to the door. Edrina was also hurrying down the hall toward the cries. A moment later Lyn ran over to him. "What happened?" she gasped.

"I don't know. Let's go and see." They started down the hall when a dragon rushed by them. Had they not been able to duck into a doorway, they might have been crushed against the wall or trampled upon.

"We'll have to wait," Greg was beginning, when an angry voice they recognized as Magior's called out loudly not far from them.

"Where are those Earth people? It is their fault. They must be punished!"

Catching hold of each other's hand, they fled in the opposite direction down the dimly-lit hall – only a torch here and there was still smoldering – around the first corner, down another hall and around another corner, and bumped into a dragoness who was coming out of a room. Lyn screamed.

"What's wrong?" said a voice with a puff of flame. "Where are you running to at this time of night?" It was the Nurse. She sounded cross but they were not afraid of her, only of Magior.

"Magior's after us!" gasped Lyn.

"We heard him looking for us," panted Greg.

"Magior! . . . Humph!" she grunted. "What is *he* doing here? Nothing good, I am sure, and what is all this commotion about?"

"We don't know! We were going to see and then heard Magior saying it was our fault and we should be punished!"

"Get behind those baskets while I go and see what has happened," said the Nurse, pushing them into the room and with a flame indicating the place. "I do not think you are in any danger; the King would not permit it. But stay there anyway until I come back."

The baskets were of the same type as found in all the sleeping rooms. The largest were fully tall enough to hide them if they sat down. They pulled the baskets out from the wall just far enough for them to squeeze behind, "But not far enough to look suspicious," said Greg.

They sat back-to-back with their arms around their knees. In this way, by turning their heads a little, they could speak to each other in the lowest of whispers; but for a long time they did not dare to make a sound. Through the open doorway they heard dragons and Dragon-Cousins – it was easy to tell the sound of them apart – hurriedly passing and re-passing, and once they heard loud voices that appeared to come from the royal quarters.

At length the commotion died down. They were horribly uncomfortable and cramped but did not dare come out. "Do you think something has happened to the Nurse?" Lyn whispered anxiously, as the darkness lessened and the piece of ceiling above their heads turned a faint gray.

"More likely she has forgotten us or knows it's not safe for us to be seen. If we knew where we were in the palace we could try to get out."

"Shhh, someone is coming."

A Dragon-Cousin stopped at the doorway, paused and then entered. They held their breath as the scuffling came towards them. Katanga's head peered around the baskets.

"Come out. Damor is looking for you. Nurse told us you were here."

Stiff, weary and frightened, they crept out.

"What has happened?" Greg asked fearfully.

"The King has gone Home," Katanga said gravely. "He was poisoned!"

Lyn gave a cry of dismay and Greg tried to smother his.

"The poison was in the potion the King takes to dull his pain. It is made of such bitter herbs the King would not have noticed the difference. When Orimalgon brought it, the King did not wish to take it at once, so Orimalgon went to the room nearby where he sleeps. Shortly after the King drank it, he cried out that he had been poisoned. The Queen, who was in the next room, called for help and Orimalgon rushed in. He could do nothing and the King went to the Blue Road before Damor and the Princess could be summoned. That is when the Queen roused the palace with her cries."

"Do they know who did it?"

"No, Orimalgon may have known or at least guessed, but he was slain, vilely slain, by Magior."

"Magior!" exclaimed the twins together.

"Yes, he claimed he had just arrived and came to the King, even though it was so late, because he had heard of a plot against the King's life and wished to warn him. He said he saw Orimalgon pause before carrying in the potion and pour something into it. He thought nothing of it at the time and waited until Orimalgon left before going in to the King. 'You lie!' Orimalgon began to say, when Magior leapt upon him and slew him with one stroke, crying out in a fury that was well-feigned, I think, that *there* was the slayer of his beloved King.

"Damor would have slain him in turn, but the Queen and the Princess threw themselves between them. Damor called for the warriors, but before they arrived, Magior was gone, crying out as he went that Orimalgon had indeed poisoned the King but it was Damor who planned it, and that he, Magior, would see that justice was done."

"Then I did see Magior!" Lyn exclaimed. "He *didn't* just arrive: he was here this afternoon hiding in that storeroom by the kitchen. He could easily have poisoned the King's drink. It was right there in the kitchen."

"And one of the assistant cooks, the one with the four lines and three big patches on his back, was with him," broke in Greg excitedly.

"That is probably why he came over and talked with us," interrupted Lyn in her turn, "so as to make certain we didn't get curious and look into the room. Why, the assistant cook could have put the poison in any time the pot was simmering in the kitchen."

81

"What do you mean?" Katanga exclaimed sharply. They explained what had happened in the courtyard.

"You must come with me at once. Damor has summoned a Council and there you must tell your tale. This will clear Orimalgon, not that Damor or Edrina or anyone else believes it, but still it is good that he will be cleared beyond any suspicion. Now I am certain he knew who poisoned the King and for this reason Magior slew him."

"Damor, is he King now?" asked Greg as they hurried to the Council room.

"Yes, immediately upon his father's death, and he will need all the help and wisdom the wisest heads in the realm can give him, for I foresee hard times for the kingdom. There can be no doubt that Magior and his Dark friend, Wondan, will do their best to take advantage of our troubles. Yes, and worse, to sow all the suspicion they can against Damor as well as create discord, if they are able, among the Green Dragons."

"What a great King his father might have been," said Lyn sadly, thinking of how he had changed. "If only he had tried sooner."

"Yes, if only he had tried sooner – but let us at least take comfort in remembering the strength of purpose and sureness of heart he showed in his last days," said Katanga.

CHAPTER 5
The Old Master

They stopped at the door of the Council room. It was full of dragons and Dragon-Cousins, as Damor had summoned, besides the regular Councillors, several others whose wisdom and experience he thought would help him. The Captain was among them, so was Edrina. The Queen was not. The room was so full, Greg feared they might be crushed should a dragon not notice them and move suddenly. He mentioned this to Katanga, adding, "I know no one would mean to hurt us, but they might."

"Wait," said Katanga. At the next silence he called out loudly, and Dragon-Cousins *can* call almost as loudly as a dragon if they need to, "Sire, it is I, Katanga, and the Children from Earth. What they have to tell will shed much light on His Majesty's death, and will, I think," (he said this with obvious satisfaction), "completely clear Orimalgon from all suspicion."

Damor was seated at the head of a large table. Lying in front of him was his father's ruby and gold collar. "None suspect Orimalgon, Katanga," he said firmly. "His love and long, devoted care of my father have made him above suspicion. Let Lyn and Greg come forward and tell what they know, for great is my grief for my father, and I would bring his slayer to justice as speedily as possible."

The dragons by the door moved aside so that Lyn and Greg could go right up to the table. Katanga had been right; Lyn saw that at once. There was already something different about Damor. His eyes showed sorrow and anger and weariness, but there was also something more: a new power that seemed to come from deep within and hung about him like an aura.

All present listened silently, though with some angry tail-lashing – in a limited way of course, the room being so crowded. At the end there were angry mutterings from all present. A Dragon-Cousin, the head of the large community whose homes were behind the palace, spoke of his mortification that one of his own should have been involved in such a heinous deed, and left to find the assistant cook and bring him to justice.

"Dragons and Dragon-Cousins, we are both to blame," Damor said kindly to him as he went out. "In the end, my heart warns me that it is we dragons who will have to bear the burden of blame for this deed and for all that I fear may happen in its wake."

"I fear you are right, Sire," said the oldest (and he was *very* old) of the dragons present. "Never have I known such treachery to occur among the Green Dragons. Wrong I have seen done, and once a dragon went over to the Dark ones, but never have I known a Green Dragon to plot evil against his own. Though, indeed, such things have happened occasionally in our long history."

"True," answered Damor, "and yet have we not

brought it upon ourselves, as Nimeon the Great warned might happen?"

"Yes," was the general answer with much sorrowful nodding of heads.

Lyn, who was given to excusing herself, was much impressed at their straightforward acceptance of blame. But that is the way with the Green Dragons. Once they realize they are in the wrong, they accept the results of their negligence and never try to shift the blame.

Damor looked so sorrowful that Lyn, forgetting where she was, tried to comfort him.

"Wasn't it mostly due to past . . . uh . . . uh . . . faulty government?" She did not want to mention his father openly.

"My father and grandfather and great-grandfather, you mean," Damor said quietly. "Yes, much was their fault. Yet each dragon and dragoness knows the laws of the Great One and of the kingdom and has listened to the Master's teachings, even if not as frequently as they should have. Each make their own choice. Now that evil times, I fear, have come upon us, we shall find out how many have made the right choice."

"Or will make it, when they are roused to see that such a choice has to be made," added the old Councillor.

"Yes, many have grown lethargic in their security and may have a bitter awakening," said a dragon in the back.

"Yet," said Damor, sitting erect with the aura of kingliness more than ever about him, "if by striving to repair the evils caused by our past negligence we can once again become what we Green Dragons should be, no price will be too great."

The room was silent, but all nodded gravely. Greg leaned over and whispered in Katanga's ear, "What a wonderful King he is!"

Katanga said proudly, "Yes, my beloved Prince Damor will be a great King."

Much discussion followed. The head Dragon-Cousin returned with a dragon, one of the palace guard. The assistant cook could not be found, he reported, but the guard had evidence to give.

"Late last night when I was on the tower keeping watch, a dragon flew off whose silhouette showed he carried a Dragon-Cousin. I challenged him. It was Magior. He said he had come to the King with a message of the greatest importance and was now carrying to the Healers a friend who had suddenly been taken very ill. Since I recognized both of them and had no reason to suspect either, I let them go on their way."

There was further discussion. The general opinion was that Magior and his accomplice were safely over the border by now, and justice would have to be delayed for the moment.

"Eventually they will return," said the Captain, "for I think this is only the beginning of their plotting."

In the meantime the dragons present decided that Damor should follow the old custom of having the King "fly the border" – their expression for flying the whole length of the border from the top to the bottom of the realm. The Captain and some of the palace warriors would go with him and they would stop at the three main garrisons and at the smaller posts in between. At each one the Captain would proclaim him the new King. Damor would speak to the warriors, collectively and then singly, and receive each warrior's oath of allegiance. Generally, this was a formality.

"In this case, however," said the Captain, "we must do all in our power to strengthen the bond that should always exist between every warrior and his King."

Another dragon spoke. "Sire, this is a sorrowful question, and yet it must be asked. What about the Queen? Why is she not here as she should be? And what knowledge does she have of our King's death?"

Damor did not reply for a long time, then he said sadly, "I do not know, nor do I know why she refused to come to this Council. She claimed she was too ill, but I doubt that is the whole reason."

Edrina spoke for the first time. "My brother, I do not think that our Dar-mother had any previous knowledge of this villainous plot against our father. I think, though, that she suspects her brother, for I left her weeping and trembling. I also think she knows herself to be a pawn in her brother's hands and refused to come so that she could tell him nothing of our plans. This will undoubtedly anger him since he must expect to be able to force her to give him information."

"The princess is undoubtedly correct, and we are fortunate the Queen would not come," commented the Captain grimly. "This is an added reason why the King should fly the border at once and return to the palace as swiftly as he can. Magior will very likely expect him to wait a few days, as is usually done, before leaving the palace, and so King Damor will be back before Magior tries to get to the Queen."

Before the Council ended, Damor, at the urging of the Councillors, put on the royal collar. "Though I would have preferred to wait," he said half to himself. As he dismissed the gathering with the customary phrase, "I thank you for your wisdom and counsel," from far overhead came the long cry of the dragon on the highest tower signaling the sunrise. "The Messenger Dragons are already proclaiming my father's death and many may come to speak with me, so I shall remain on the terrace as long as necessary before leaving," Damor decided.

He was right. Many did come, among them the Prince of the Dragon-Cousins, brought from his principality in the south on the back of a dragon. Damor conferred with him a long time and invited him to stay at the palace, but the Prince refused saying, "I may be needed in my own realm. Magior has often been among us. He was never liked, but it may be that some have listened too long to his sweet and smooth words and been taken in by them," and off he went on his dragon, clinging to a type of padded harness which the dragons wear when carrying their wingless, low-slung friends.

At length Damor was free to leave. He first spoke to Greg and Lyn who were sitting disconsolately in a corner of the terrace, feeling more than ever in the way. "Do not be troubled, but stay with us, I beg you, if your hearts give you the courage to do so; for that, I think, is what you are meant to do, as I have told you before. Besides, the sight of you fills my own heart with hope, for I am sure you were not sent as a sign of our downfall."

"It is odd," Greg commented to his sister, "how Damor always insists that we were sent. Just as his father insisted that we would also find out our own reason why we are here. I don't see why they think that way. We could have chosen not to come through the Door. I don't know how the Door got there, but I *do* know we could be sitting on the sand in the cave right now instead of being here."

"Perhaps we were given the chance to choose to do the right thing," Lyn said thoughtfully. "Don't tell me you wish you hadn't come?"

"No!" Greg said quickly, and deep inside he knew he had to find the reason why they were there or he would never have peace of mind again.

Damor flew off accompanied by most of the palace warriors who acted as an honor guard. During his short absence the First Councillor would handle any urgent matters. Edrina was to take charge of the palace as the Queen could do nothing. "I shall return as quickly as I can," Damor said to her, "but it will not be before the third or fourth day, as I must listen fully to each warrior lest I seem to slight one."

That afternoon and the next day passed quietly. The Queen did not appear. She refused to remain next to the room where the King had been poisoned and moved with her child to other rooms, one of which opened on to the terrace. On the third day, shortly after sunrise, the twins were already having breakfast outside and chatting merrily with Edrina and the Councillor they had met the first night, when they heard a familiar voice, and, to their terror, Magior came out of the Queen's rooms.

Edrina drew herself up. "What are you doing here?" she demanded. "Are you not afraid to be brought to justice for the murder of Orimalgon? Or do you come to give yourself up willingly to the judgment of the King and his Council?"

Magior settled himself comfortably, and insolently said, "The King is dead. Your brother is not fit to rule, much less to administer justice, as all will soon agree." He gave a malevolent chuckle. "You, my dear Princess, are not of age; and so, no matter what your brother may have said, the Queen, because of her greater age and wisdom," he gave another and grimmer chuckle, "surely is the one in charge. She says I may remain. In fact, I think I shall return to her now and give her further advice." At the door he turned around. "By the way, my dear Princess, are you coming to the Gathering that is taking place today at the Field of Celebration just before high noon?"

"Gathering at the Field of Celebration!" exclaimed Edrina in astonishment. "What do you mean? My brother, King Damor, has not called for a Gathering of the dragons."

"No, he would not dare do so. The Master has called the Gathering. Justice shall be done today whether your brother wishes it or not." He vanished into the building.

"What does he mean? And how does he dare come here?" Edrina said indignantly to the Councillor. "He knows he will be brought to justice. I shall have him seized." She hesitated. "Damor left only four older members of the guard. Magior is a fierce warrior and I do not want any slain while I am in charge."

The old Councillor thought a while. "Do nothing for the moment. Magior must know how few warriors are here and perhaps he has friends among them, or else why did not the guard on the tower cry a warning?"

"That is my fault. Since they are so few, I told the guard they need not keep watch during the morning hours. I thought there would be no danger with so many coming and going. I will send word immediately for the guard to go on duty," which she did.

The Councillor again thought a long while before saying, "Go to the Gathering and see what is happening. You may be needed to speak in your brother's defense, as I am certain that this Gathering has been carefully planned to take place when he cannot be there."

"Don't you think the Master has sent word to Damor?" Greg asked. He remembered the Master's eyes and could not imagine him doing anything underhanded.

"I do not for a moment believe the Master called this Gathering," the Councillor replied gravely. "In fact, I shall fly myself right now to the Mount to make certain he knows about it. You, Princess, send word to the King to return as swiftly as he can . . . with the warriors."

The Princess sent off a dragoness, the wife of one of the palace guard, with the message, and said to

Greg, "She is very swift, and if we are being spied upon, as we must be – or how else would Magior know when to come? – she may not be suspected as she often visits her brother who is with the Border Guard."

Near noon, the Nurse came onto the terrace and said to Edrina in a low voice, "I came across Magior in the Jewel Chamber. He was looking at the Coronation Collars. When I asked him what he was doing, he gave a start and said he was just making certain that they did not need polishing. I sat there until he left, which annoyed him. I think they should be removed and hidden where he cannot find them until the King returns and decides what to do."

"How shall we do it?" Edrina was puzzled. "No one must see us doing it since I no longer know whom to trust. Baskets would arouse suspicion and we could not prevent Magior from examining them. He is too strong."

"Hide them in your bed," Lyn suggested.

"That would be promptly searched," Edrina replied.

Various spots were considered and rejected as neither Edrina nor the Nurse felt that any place in the palace was safe.

"Wait!" Edrina exclaimed, but softly. "I know what we can do. What is the name of those things you take on and off?"

"You mean our jackets?" Greg said with a laugh.

"Yes. You can put the Coronation Collars around you and cover them with your jackets."

"It might work," Lyn agreed, laughing also. "But

they will bulge out and look as though something were under them."

"That will not matter," Greg chimed in. "No one here knows what they are supposed to look like. We haven't worn them since we came, and so only you and Damor have seen them. Others will think they are part of us. Is there any fear of our being seen taking the collars?"

"The entrance to the Jewel Chamber can be seen by anyone coming out of the rooms the Queen now occupies," the Nurse reminded Edrina.

"I will go there and seem to speak earnestly with Magior. In the meantime, Nurse, you take Lyn and Greg to the Jewel Chamber. After they have the collars, take them at once to the Master and ask him what to do with them. I shall go to the Gathering as soon as I think you are well away from the palace."

"Do you think Damor will come soon?" Greg asked.

"That depends on how long it takes for him to get the message. We do not know where he is along the border."

The twins ran to get their jackets and put them on. They followed Edrina at a distance until she motioned them to stop. The nurse was waiting. As soon as she saw the Princess disappear into a room, she signaled and they ran up to her.

"Go in there quickly," she said. "The Coronation Collars are in the center chest. Try to get the second-best also. They are in the chest to the right."

They darted in, expecting shelves full of jewels. There was nothing to be seen except four chests and a small carrying basket in one corner. Greg lifted the lid of the center chest and stood staring.

"Look at that!" Lyn breathed in an excited whisper. The bottom of the chest was lined with a white fur and on it were two collars at least a foot wide and blazing with jewels.

"Hurry," urged the Nurse. Greg lifted out the largest, which was studded with rubies, emeralds and diamonds, and clasped it around his waist. Lyn did the same around her waist with the somewhat smaller Queen's collar of sapphires and diamonds. It was heavy.

"Shut the chest," ordered the Nurse. "Now take the second-best." These were the collars they had seen the first night.

"Pull your shirt over the first one so they will not scratch each other," whispered Lyn, doing her best to get her blouse over the Queen's collar. She put the second-best over that and tried to get her jacket on. "I can't possibly get my jacket over both of them," she said, struggling vigorously.

"I can't either," said Greg, also struggling.

The Nurse glanced both ways down the hall. It was empty. "Take that basket there in the corner and put everything else in it. I won't have that Magior getting hold of anything."

They piled the second-best collars in, padded them well with furs, and then opened the other chests. There was not as much as they had expected: two more pairs of much less elaborate collars, bracelets for the Queen, and extra gold and silver chains should a King have several children and grandchildren.

"Close the chests so that everything looks the

same. Quick now."

She put the basket around her neck and led the way swiftly down the hall. Behind them could be heard Edrina, speaking loudly and rapidly. The Nurse stopped at a small, dark room in the back part of the palace. It was full of broken baskets and odds and ends. "Things waiting to be mended," she said, and buried the basket at the very back under everything. "I will hide it later."

They left by a side door and followed the Nurse a good way from the palace before she halted beneath a large cluster of trees.

"Unless Magior is actually in the air, he will not see us leave from here," she said.

"Oooh! I can't get up," panted Lyn as she tried to scramble onto the Nurse's back and slipped down. "I can't bend! It's like being in a cast."

"Here, I'll boost you up." Greg got her up and then with her help managed to climb up behind her with many an "Ouch!" as the points of the jewelled collar stabbed into him.

The Nurse had only taken a few wingbeats when the dragon sentinel called loudly from the tower: "Beware! Beware! Dark Dragons coming! Six of them!"

The Nurse shot forward with a jolt that nearly unseated them, looking backward over her shoulder as she did so. "Edrina! Edrina!" she screamed. "Be swift! Be swift!"

They saw Edrina leap into the air calling to all the dragons in the palace to flee. Magior was right behind her. He tried to knock her down, but she was too quick for him and with a glance at the

Nurse, she sped off in the opposite direction. Four of the Dark Dragons attacked the palace warriors and two at Magior's bidding raced with him after the Princess.

"We must reach the Mount before they are free to follow us," said the Nurse. "Tell me if I go too fast for you."

They had to pass near the Field of Celebration where dragons were already gathering. Not many had yet arrived.

"Look at all the Dark Dragons among the Green ones," said Greg.

"I see them," replied the Nurse. "I also see the Master who is landing this moment. I must tell him about the attack and Magior's further treachery."

She circled down and landed on the raised, grass-covered dais at one end beside the Master of Wisdom. She spoke rapidly and explained in a low voice what had happened. The Master listened intently, then said, "Stay near so as to see what happens and bring word of it as swiftly as you can to the King. Hide the Children from Earth."

The Nurse crawled down the side of the dais which was so steep that Lyn lost her hold and slid forward onto the Nurse's neck, then off onto the ground, with Greg on top of her. The grass was soft but the Collar jabbed into her more than ever. She did not have time to think about it because the Nurse, who had swung around facing the dais, said, "Quick, under my wings." She spread them slightly and they ducked under, one on each side, then she closed her wings over them as she would have over small dragons and settled herself. It was terribly hot and uncomfortable under her wings. "You can see what's happening," she said, opening them a trifle, "but don't let yourselves be seen." Lyn was under the wing on the far side of the dais, so she could not see much, but Greg had a clear view of all that followed.

The dragons were restless and several called out, "Master, why have you summoned us?" "Where is the King?" "Why are there so many Dark Dragons here? We thought they had been expelled."

The Master sat up and a respectful silence fell. Even the Dark Dragons did not dare interrupt.

"I did not summon you, and the Dark Dragons are here without the King's knowledge," he was beginning, when Magior and Wondan landed on the dais a little behind the Master. After them came the Queen with a carrying basket around her neck. She landed near her brother and remained huddled at the edge of the dais, looking miserable.

"I summoned the Gathering," Magior interrupted the Master.

"Be silent!" called out a dragoness loudly. Greg recognized her as one of the Healers who lived on the Mount. "It is for the Master to speak."

Magior made a pretense of bowing respectfully to the Master. Never had his voice been oilier or smoother. "Certainly, we must all listen to our *last*" (he emphasized the word) "Master of Wisdom. Let me, though, first explain the terrible necessity that drove me to call this Gathering in our great Master's name. As you have all heard, I am certain, our beloved late King was poisoned by one whom he trusted completely, the Dragon-Cousin Orimalgon. I saw him pour something into the potion he made regularly for the King, and His Majesty drank it, unsuspecting of any treachery. I was waiting to speak with His Majesty and dashed in when I heard him cry out that he was poisoned, only to find him dying. With his last words he accused Orimalgon. In my desperate grief I may have overreached justice, as I slew Orimalgon on the spot, so great was my horror at the deed.

"Now I come to the most grievous part of my account which I tell with sorrow and only because I so love justice. I had come to the King that very night to warn him of a plot I had heard against him, a plot – alas, that I should have to say this! – planned by his own son, Damor, who was weary of waiting to come to the Kingship.

"Surely by this heinous crime, he has not only forfeited his right to be King, but should be driven from the kingdom. In his place, our beloved King's second son should be declared King, and for this purpose the Queen has brought him." She made no move, and so Magior took the basket and lifted from it a baby dragon and held it up for all to see. "Indeed, I would have urged that he be crowned on this day, but the Coronation Collars have been stolen – at Damor's instigation, no doubt – and probably by his friends, those wretched children from that place called Earth.

"Master, you have heard my words and see yonder Dragon-Cousin," he continued, indicating the assistant cook who was nearby in the front rank, "who was with me and is a second witness."

The Dragon-Cousin nodded vigorously and said

loudly, "I saw it all."

"Will you not, beloved Master of Wisdom, proclaim this Prince to be our new King, instead of the vile Damor?" Magior concluded.

All present looked at the old Master of Wisdom. He drew himself up and his voice, when he spoke, was far stronger and clearer than Greg would have thought possible in one so old. But he did not answer Magior. Instead, he turned, looked straight at the Queen, and said, "What does the Queen have to say?"

The Queen's head had dropped down towards the ground during her brother's speech. She trembled a moment more, then raised her head, looked straight at the Master and said simply, "This is not the King's son. Our child caught cold and went Home last night. And it was not Orimalgon who poisoned the King."

"Fool!" screamed her brother, blowing a blast of flame that caught her on the side. With a shriek she shot off the dais and flew away crying.

"Here is the fool!" roared Wondan, leaping upon the Master and ripping him with his talons. "Let this be the end of this Master business! Now learn to live in freedom like us!"

A roar of rage rose from the assembly but broke off as the dying Master lifted his head and called out, "You still have a Master, O Green Dragons, for the Young Master lives!"

Then he collapsed. The dragoness who had spoken previously rushed to his side and cried out in her turn, "Yes! The Young Master did not die!"

Wondan lunged at her, but the assembled dragons were in the air. A dragon dived at him and he had to defend himself. In a moment all was pandemonium. On the ground the Dragon-Cousins bumped into each other trying to get out of the fighting dragons' way, who at times came so low that their tails swept the ground. Overhead, the Dark and Green Dragons were locked in combat. Through the tumult could be heard the dragonesses urging their children away, as the Dark fighters were striking indiscriminately at the dragonesses and children. One youngster was too slow, and though his mother tried to get between him and a fighting pair, the wings of one of them struck him and he fell with a cry. Too late, his mother flung herself after him, and Lyn covered her eyes so as not to see the little dragon hit the ground. Only a few of the Green Dragons present were warriors. They were fighting valiantly but were being overpowered by their Dark foes, when suddenly the Green Dragons' battle cry rang out: "For the Great One and the King!" Damor and his warriors had arrived.

Now the Dark Dragons were outnumbered. The sky rang with cries, and streaks of flame shot through the smoke surrounding the combatants. The Dark warriors began to retreat and the battle moved farther away.

"On my back, quickly!" cried the Nurse. "No one will notice us now!"

"What about the baby?" cried Lyn as they took off and she saw the frightened little thing running about the empty platform.

The Nurse hesitated a moment, then went on, saying, "I will have someone come back for him."

"Where is the Master?" Greg asked, looking around in astonishment. He could not imagine how he could have been rescued so quickly.

"He went to the Blue Road while you were watching the attack."

She landed at the edge of the nearest forest. "There, you can go by yourself to the Mount. It is only a short way. I must get back to my nursling," she said, meaning the Princess Edrina.

"Do you think she was caught?"

"Yes, I saw it, and fear that in the struggle she may have been hurt and needs my care." And off she went, ignoring the twins' pleas to be taken to the Mount.

"She may think it a short distance to the Mount," Greg said ruefully, "but I saw how far it was as we came down and it's a good, long walk."

They stood out of sight under the trees watching the fighting that was getting farther and farther away. The Dark Dragons appeared to be in full flight.

"Well, that's over," said Lyn with a sigh of relief. "I hope Damor will be able to free Edrina quickly."

For a while they remained at the forest's edge, hoping to catch the attention of a friendly dragon who would carry them to the Mount, but saw none. All they saw was a dragon or dragoness, it was too far to tell which, dropping onto the distant dais and flying off again with a carrying basket.

"I am glad the Nurse remembered to send someone for the baby. I was afraid she would forget," said Lyn as they went into the forest.

At first there was little undergrowth, and a narrow, hard-beaten Dragon-Cousin path that was easy to follow, but shortly, it went off in the wrong direction. After an hour or so the forest thickened and the underbrush grew fairly heavy. They avoided having to push through it as much as they could by ducking around the clumps, until they came out into a meadow and saw with dismay that they were going in the wrong direction.

"We'll have to beat our way as straight through as we can, whether it's hard going or not," said Greg, "and when we come to a meadow we'll have to go around it, or else we would be at the mercy of any Dark Dragon who caught us out in the open."

Lyn agreed wearily. "It's not the walking I mind, but this heavy collar. I've loosened it so that it hangs down over my hips, but it bangs against me and I'm afraid of damaging it, or knocking out one of those enormous jewels."

"Let's try hanging them over our shoulders with our jackets on top. That should protect them and keep them pretty much hidden."

The change did make the collars easier to carry, but they grew heavier and heavier, and the forest hotter and hotter, as the afternoon wore on. At last Lyn sank down and took off the Queen's collar.

"Isn't there anywhere we can hide them? If there were a clear landmark, the dragons could easily find them."

"That's a good idea, Lyn, and it must be a landmark easily seen from the air."

A short distance further they came to a meadow through which a small river snaked, forming two pools as it went. The twins decided this was an ex-

102

cellent landmark. They chose a spot on the edge of the field between two white-trunked trees, wrapped the collars carefully in their jackets and covered them with leaves and loose branches.

Lyn laughed. "I almost feel like a thief in a story, hiding the stolen jewels. I hope Damor isn't annoyed at our leaving them here."

"Can't help it if he is. We have to get to the Mount before nightfall, and it's a long way yet."

Nightfall found them panting and struggling through the underbrush of the rough slope that led up to the base of the Mount. They kept on until it was too dark to see the way, then sat down and rested until the rising moon gave them enough light to continue. Above loomed the Mount. Its sides were steep and covered with trees through which the moonlight filtered.

"I think we must have taken the steepest route," said Greg as he caught hold of a bush to help himself up, and then held out his hand to his sister.

She stopped suddenly. "Oh! My purse! Remember, after my dunking I put it in my jacket pocket for safety? I forgot to take it out again; I suppose I've lost it this time," she said ruefully.

About halfway up they took a long rest and were about to start again when Lyn whispered, "Shhh . . . what's that?" From not far to the right of them came a long, rustling sound. They froze as it came nearer and nearer, and gave a joint sigh of relief when it veered off and grew fainter.

"Must be snakes. Damor mentioned them once," Greg said. They listened, then went on cautiously, stopping to listen every now and then. Soon the sound came once more. Again it was on the right, though not as close this time, and again it passed and faded. Then there was a long silence. As the sky turned gray, the noise came again and with it, voices.

"Oh!" exclaimed Lyn with a cry of relief. "It must be a Dragon-Cousin path to the top. Why didn't we think of it sooner? We wouldn't have had all this struggling."

"Be careful," Greg said, trying to hold her back. She broke away and pushed through to what was indeed a path along which two Dragon-Cousins were making their way to the top, which they assured her was only a little farther on.

The morning clouds were growing a bright pink when they climbed onto the plateau. It was filled with dragons, mostly warriors. Damor was easily recognizable by his ruby collar.

Crying happily, "Damor! Damor!" they ran over to him and Lyn hugged him. He was equally happy to see them.

"How relieved I am to have you safe with me!" he said, gently touching her with his head. "I have been so worried about you! A dragoness saw you on the Nurse's back when the palace was attacked, but she did not know if you had been pursued, and no one else has been able to tell me where you were or what had happened to you. One elderly dragon thought he had seen you for a moment at the Gathering. Then I worried more than ever, because I knew both Magior and Wondan were searching for you, and if they had caught you they would have slain you at once. Wondan, at least, will trouble us no more. The Captain slew him."

"No, the King slew him in the end," the Captain broke in. "I only helped. And it was His Majesty's first combat," he said proudly.

"Are the Dark Dragons all driven from the kingdom?" Greg asked eagerly.

Damor shook his head. "No," he said, "the Dark King and his warriors hold the palace. It must have been part of their plot while I was away and Magior called the Gathering. None of us suspected how closely they must have been watching my movements. Nor did any think for a moment that the palace would be attacked; it is so far from the border that we looked upon it as safe. Ah! That evil pair, Wondan and Magior! What harm their treachery has already done us – and more is yet to come."

"Edrina?" Lyn asked anxiously.

"She is held captive. The dragoness who brought me the news said she did not think she was hurt, as she flew back to the palace between her captors, defying them at every wingbeat. Because of her and the others who are also held captive, we dare not storm the palace; they would all be slain at once. Nor do we think she is in any danger at the moment; she is too valuable a hostage. If only we knew how many were in the plot, or . . ." (with a deep sigh) "who are the ones we cannot trust."

"Did you hear what happened at the Field of Celebration?" asked Greg.

"Yes, the treacherous slaying of the Master of Wisdom and the base attack on dragonesses and children. For that evil deed we repaid them, and only two of those despicable warriors returned to their own land."

"What happened to Magior?" said Greg.

"Unfortunately he was one of those who escaped; but in the end, he will not escape us."

"Is it true that the Young Master is alive?" Lyn asked eagerly, looking all around trying to see him.

"Yes. Had he been a warrior he would surely have been slain, but the Masters never fight. He dropped to the ground at once, and so his attacker missed giving him a mortal stroke, though the wound he did give was deep and grievous. Had our warriors not seen the attack and come to his aid at once, he would have bled to death. I do not know how the rumor spread that he had gone Home. But it was well that it did, and that is why my father silenced me when we returned that day from the Mount. He saw at once it might be to our advantage for our foes to think their evil deed had succeeded. He hoped it would make them overconfident. Now they know they failed: the Master lives. There must be many bitter recriminations and accusations among them. But we Green Dragons, though hard times have come upon us, rejoice: for we still have a Master!" he ended triumphantly.

"Wasn't the Queen brave?" Lyn said softly. "She cleared you completely and showed up her brother's treachery."

"Yes," said Damor, "she could live with unhappiness, but she could never live with a lie. No true Green Dragon could."

"And the Master knew it," Greg said reflectively.

"Yes, the Master knew it," agreed Damor.

106

CHAPTER 6
Behind the Palace

Damor only laughed when told about the Coronation Collars having been left hidden under the trees. "You were brave to try to save them. It would have gone hard with you had you been caught. They may be only a symbol of the kingship, but they are an important symbol. I would have hated to know the Dark King had them."

Two young warriors with a carrying basket well lined with furs were sent to find them, which they did easily. They brought back the wet and muddy jackets as well. Lyn was relieved to find her purse still safely tucked in a corner of her pocket. "I'm going to get that book after all," she said with a laugh to Greg.

In the next few days Damor told the tale many times with much chuckling. Then Lyn and Greg had to put the jackets on and take them off every time Damor told the story in order to show the audience how they had carried off the collars practically under Magior's nose. This moment, however, was not one for telling stories. The situation was tense and there were many decisions for Damor to make.

"Are you going to make the Mount your headquarters?" Greg asked.

"No," said Damor. "True, it would be easy to defend, but our every flight could be seen from the palace tower. We came here to guard the Master and the others who have taken refuge here. Tonight between nightfall and moonrise, we shall remove him to a safer place, and there, for the moment at least, will be our headquarters."

"I suppose the best place from which to defend the realm would be in those mountains," Greg continued, pointing to the north which was mountainous, "rather than in the south where there are only a few hills. You could swoop down on the enemy while they would have to fly up to attack."

"You have a good warrior's eye," Damor said approvingly. "But that would leave our Dragon-Cousins' country unprotected. They would be slaughtered or enslaved. No, we shall defend a line across the kingdom, south of this Mount. Swift messengers have been sent to warn all who live in the north to leave their homes before they are attacked. I fear, though, that some have lived for so many passings in security, that they will delay overlong. The warriors alone will remain at their posts. We do not think it likely the Dark Dragons will try to capture that area. Our best herds and fields are in the center and south of the kingdom."

Lyn found the Young Master, now the Master, resting in a house through whose open door the sea and the Blue Road could be seen. His eyes, like Damor's, had a new power in them and for a moment Lyn was hesitant to disturb him. He noticed her hesitation and welcomed her warmly, calling her his "new friend." When told about the collars, he nodded approvingly. "It is good they were saved from those who want them only for evil purposes."

"Yes, they must be fantastically valuable," commented Lyn.

He did not understand, and she explained what she meant by valuable.

"No," said the Master. "In that way, for us they have no value. Their value lies in the love with which the gift was given. For the friendship between the first King of the Green Dragons who came here and the Dragon-Cousin Prince was so great, it is still remembered in our tales, as are the deeds of the long line of Kings who have worn the collars."

For a long time Lyn sat quietly content beside the Master until one of the Healers ordered her away, saying the Master had to have his wounds dressed – they were almost healed – and then must rest.

Later, Greg came upon her sitting on top of a Dragon-Cousin house, out of the way of the milling dragons. She was looking at the Blue Road.

"Do you know, Greg," she said with a choke in her voice, "if Mother fell ill again and went Home as she nearly did, I wouldn't feel quite so badly after seeing the Blue Road. It is so beautiful."

Lyn had never been considered pretty. Now her face was so transformed by an inner light that she was nearly beautiful. For a long moment Greg could not take his eyes off her; then he turned and for the first time really looked at the Blue Road.

At intervals during the day, small groups of dragons were sent southward, escorted part way by warriors who then returned for another group. As soon as it was dark the Master was carried off. Then began the total evacuation of the Mount. The sick and wounded and elderly were taken in convoy far south. All during the day, the various stores of dried and fresh herbs and roots, pots of prepared ointments, food, and various implements used by the Healers had been carefully packed in baskets. When the warriors returned, dragonesses slid their necks through the carrying straps and flew off. Some of them carried Dragon-Cousins on their backs, but most of the Dragon-Cousins who lived on the Mount or who had taken refuge there, just vanished over the edge of the plateau down their own paths. Katanga was one of the last to leave.

"Is there any danger of your being caught?" Lyn asked him.

"Not my people," said Katanga with a laugh. "Once we are in a forest, even a thin one, we can slip from tree to tree and shrub to shrub without being seen from the air. Besides, look at all these warriors. If they saw us being attacked, they would attack in return."

"Are you really so confident the dragons will always help you?" Greg asked curiously, remembering all the broken treaties and sworn allies who became enemies in his Earth's short history.

"They have never failed us," said Katanga firmly. He added reproachfully, "And how could you think even for a moment that Damor, of all dragons, would desert us?"

A Dragon-Cousin told Katanga that all was ready. "Farewell!" he cried. "I am leaving; I shall see you tomorrow," and he slid over the edge with his friend.

Greg was standing by Damor, who was about to

order the final departure, when several dragon families arrived together. In the ensuing confusion, Greg was in real danger of being inadvertently stepped on. He darted through the milling group, dodging wings and tails, back to the low rooftop where Lyn had prudently remained. Even there they were not safe, as a dragon, not noticing them, narrowly missed knocking them off with his head. Above them was the overhanging branch of a shade tree. "Up there we'll be safer," said Lyn. She could just reach it and with help from her brother swung herself up; he climbed up beside her. They could not see as well from there, but they could hear Damor and the Captain ordering the dragon families to fly to various locations in the defended area. These commands were followed by a tremendous beating of many wings and then silence. After the silence had lasted a good while, Greg and Lyn realized with sinking hearts that they were alone on the Mount. They had been forgotten.

"I'm sure they will come back for us," said Lyn, trying to bolster her fading courage.

"But when? Will the Dark ones get here first?"

The moon was well up in the sky when, fearful their silhouettes would betray them to a passing enemy, they crawled to a tree near the edge of the plateau from which they could see clearly in a half-circle from north to south. Everything was calm and peaceful as though there had been no tragedy, no attack. Not a dragon was to be seen in any direction. And straight ahead lay the Blue Road, which was no longer blue, but a path of shimmering gold in the moonlight. The sight comforted Lyn.

"We'll just have to find a place to hide until Damor comes back for us," she said. "Don't you think the Dark Dragons would be less likely to search the woods on the slopes above this place than the slopes below, where Magior has undoubtedly told them are the Dragon-Cousin paths?"

"Yes." Greg felt just as confident of Damor's return as she did. "Let's see if we can find some food or rugs to make ourselves comfortable with."

They searched several of the buildings but the departing Healers had cleared out everything thoroughly. "Well, it's warm. Sleeping on the ground won't be bad," said Lyn.

It was not comfortable. Neither of them had ever slept on the bare ground before, and they spent the night dozing on and off and getting up every now and then to try to find a softer spot.

As soon as it was light enough to see fairly distinctly, they resumed their search for left-behind food, though without much hope.

"Well, well," said a voice as they came out empty-handed from a building. "What are you doing here?" It was a Dragon-Cousin.

"Were you also left behind?" said Greg, wondering if this was a friend or enemy.

"Oh my, no!" said the Dragon-Cousin cheerfully. "I volunteered to stay so as to direct any latecomers where to go."

"Aren't you afraid of the Dark Dragons attacking this place?" Lyn asked, surprised at his nonchalance.

The Dragon-Cousin, whose name was Partemegan, laughed. "Never fear their attacking this Mount. Although they hate the Master and the Blue

Road, they will not dare come here. If they want to find out anything they will send a Green Dragon, but I doubt if he will find this spot to his liking either, not anymore."

Where the rising slope met the plateau, several small caves had long ago been hollowed out for use as storerooms. Their openings were protected from rain and wind by tall bushes set just far enough apart to permit a narrow opening. In the one closest to the left edge of the plateau their new friend had made his hideout. He had plenty of food which he gladly shared. "Not hot, unfortunately," he said, "because a fire is too risky. The dragons are so keen-sighted they would see the slightest curl of smoke if they were anywhere near." He showed them a little-used, partly overgrown path leading through the thickest part of the woods on the downward slope. "If any danger turns up, run down that path at once and turn to the right at the bottom which will lead you south. Keep going straight until you reach the Green warriors. I will take a good look at what is happening and then will follow," he continued as chattily as though directing them to a friend's house. He noticed Lyn glancing longingly at his comfortable bed. "Where did you sleep last night? On the ground? How uncomfortable! Just curl up on my bed. I am going to keep an eye on what is going on in the valley. If anything exciting happens, I will wake you up in time to run away."

They could not help but be reassured by his cheery manner and in a few minutes were fast asleep on his bed. Several hours later, greatly refreshed, they awoke at the sound of his bustling among his pots. "I am preparing a little midmorning something. Not as good, of course, as I would have to offer you if I were in my own home. No matter, though. Do come and share it with me." They needed no second invitation.

"Do you know," he asked as he filled their bowls, "if it is true that one of the assistant cooks at the palace was in the plot against the King? Yes? That is very sad of course, but you know the dragons' old saying, 'It is an ill flame that does not warm someone.' When this trouble is over, I think I shall apply for the place. I once saw that kitchen with its great ovens and fireplace, and ever since, I have dreamed of being a cook there. Now," he said after they had finished and had helped him with the dishes and put them away, "I have to get back to my lookout post. I am hoping to get some information about how many are at the palace and about our enemies' movements that will be of use to King Damor."

"How will you get the information to him?" Greg asked.

"On the south side away from the enemy there is a tall, slender bush rising out of a clump of lower ones. It cannot be mistaken. If I have anything to report, when the sun is highest I will shake it. A warrior will be on the lookout and will answer by circling twice. Then Damor will send a messenger at night to get my news. I will shake it today just in case he does not know you were left behind."

His lookout post was a large, heavily-leafed bush near the edge of the plateau. He had hollowed out the center of it by chewing the inner stems and so could lie unseen, watching from under the lower branches. He made them crawl on their stomachs the last few yards into its shelter. Lyn squeezed in on one side of him and Greg on the other. It was a tight fit, but Partemegan did not mind. "Glad of the company," he said and chatted away, pointing out anything he thought of interest.

To the north the towers of the palace could be seen rising above the shade trees around it. Except for a dragon every now and then arriving or departing, there was no sign of any special activity. To the south, pairs of dragons were flying back and forth.

"That must be Damor's patrol," said Greg.

"Yes, he will not be caught unprepared again, even though it is not likely the Dark villains would be such fools as to attempt an open attack on such a well-defended line," Partemegan replied.

"It was not Damor's fault," objected Lyn loyally. "He has only been King for four days."

"No, certainly. It was either the Captain's or his father's lack of foresight. And yet," he lost his cheerful manner and said in a low tone half to himself, "who could have guessed such treachery was brewing?"

Nothing happened. After a while Lyn said, "Are you as cramped as I am, Greg? Let's go back to the cave and stretch for a bit."

She was wiggling out backwards when Partemegan said, "Lie still. Here come some of the Dark ones."

A group of three flew close to the Mount and eyed it inquisitively. One of them started to land, then shied away. The largest, a huge Dark Dragon with cruel, fierce eyes and two terrible long scars like a double "S" down his gray chest landed for a moment, made a sharp sound and left at once. They flew away talking angrily.

"I told you they would not dare come here," Partemegan said triumphantly. Greg did not say anything. He had been looking at the Blue Road, he couldn't help it from where he was, and in the brief moment the huge Dark Dragon had been on the Mount, one of his great wings had come between Greg and the Blue Road, and Greg had felt as though a sudden, cold darkness had come upon him and he lay there shivering inside.

"That big one with the two terrible scars is the Dark King," said Partemegan. "It was the Captain who made those scars in a border fight some twenty passings ago."

In the afternoon a Green Dragon flew up, hesitated a moment, then landed. It was Magior. He seemed uneasy as he glanced into one or two of the empty buildings, then hastily flew off.

"Did you see?" said Lyn in a horrified whisper. "Magior has taken off his gold armband."

"I don't see how he could have kept it on," Partemegan said grimly.

Greg again felt cold inside.

No other dragon came near the Mount. Twice, Dragon-Cousins crept cautiously onto the plateau and were sent on their way after a bite to eat and an encouraging word from Partemegan.

Towards dusk, from their lookout they saw a group of dragons of different sizes, all with carrying baskets, flying as swiftly as the smallest could go, along the shore towards the south.

"Families," said Partemegan.

"I hope they are not seen," said Lyn anxiously.

"They have been. Look!" said Partemegan. Six dragons had risen from the palace grounds and were speeding towards the sea. The families were on the watch. The children landed at once on the beach. The parents dropped off their carrying baskets and turned together to defend themselves and their children. Lyn and Greg were watching with such anxious horror, they were startled to hear Partemegan's "Hoorah!" From the south coming at a terrific speed was a V-formation of Green warriors. Just in time, they swept between the Dark Dragons and the families, and with a tremendous braking of wings turned to attack. The combat was short and swift. None were slain, but a Dark Dragon had to be helped back to the palace by his comrades and Partemegan said he thought two Green ones were wounded though probably not badly from the way they flew. In the meantime the families had collected their children and belongings and reached safety.

Soon after nightfall came the sound of dragons landing.

"Lyn, Greg," called a voice. It was Damor, relieved and apologetic. "There was a mix-up in the orders. The dragoness who was supposed to have taken you thought another had done so. Partemegan, have you anything to report?"

The news about Magior was received with angry mutterings of "The Traitor." "Poisoner." "Murderer." "If only I could engage him in combat."

"Probably no one else will come here, Parte-megan," said Damor. "You can leave and join us."

Partemegan said he did not want to leave. "No, Sire," he said in his cheery way. "I shall stay here. There is just enough danger to make things interesting. If I find out anything, I shall signal as we agreed."

Damor praised and thanked him. Then he said, "Greg and Lyn, get on my back, we must be off. These warriors will guard us. We no longer fly alone," he added tersely.

Damor's headquarters were well behind the patrolled line at a place where two groups of dragon houses were fairly close together. "Not more than two wingbeats away," as the dragons say. The Master, who was rapidly recovering, was in one of the houses. Several of the Healers lived with him. The other houses were for the wounded. Behind one set of houses was a flat area on which a group of Dragon-Cousins were building ovens and open fireplaces – they are much better at that sort of thing than the dragons – so as to feed the warriors. The dragons were carrying supplies, as well as Dragon-Cousins when necessary, and lit fires; they did all the heavy work.

Damor said that the next day Greg and Lyn would be carried much farther south, but they begged to be allowed to remain. "If there is an attack we can duck into the woods."

"Very well," acquiesced Damor. "There is no real danger here." The Captain agreed, saying, "They will not attack where they know we are in full force. That is not their way. Raids, small swift attacks, are

118

what they prefer – indeed, what all dragons prefer."

"Perhaps we can be useful in some way," Greg offered.

Damor gave him a swift, keen glance. "Do you mean that?" he said.

Greg was taken aback, but answered boldly, "Yes."

"And you?" asked Damor, looking at Lyn.

She felt her throat get tight and dry, swallowed hard and said as bravely as she could, "Yes, anything to help you and Edrina. Is there any way to rescue her?"

"Not for the moment," Damor answered sadly. "The Dark King, the one you saw with the double scars on his chest, has settled himself at the palace with his" (Damor made a sound of disgust) "wives. A dragoness who was captured when the palace was attacked but not well guarded managed to escape, and told me that Edrina is unharmed except for some scratches and bruises from her resistance to capture. She is kept under guard but is treated well." He broke off abruptly. "If you want to help, I am sure the Dragon-Cousins will find plenty for you to do."

"Damor has something up his sleeve," said Lyn as they ran off, and then laughed at herself for using such a phrase.

The Dragon-Cousins were delighted to have two such dexterous helpers and kept them working until they were ready to drop.

"I couldn't lift another brick," said Lyn wearily, sitting on a half-finished oven when the call for supper was sounded. The Dragon-Cousin in charge noticed her fatigue and after supper kindly put her to work sorting herbs until nightfall. When she curled up on the piles of leaves that served as beds, she fell asleep at once. By the next afternoon, the ovens and fireplaces were ready and the supplies carefully stored and covered with heavy hides.

Two days later, the morning broke dull and gray with a drizzle that turned into a fog by noon. It was, in short, a miserable sort of day. Except for those on patrol duty, the dragons lay under the thickest trees and the Dragon-Cousins, who hate wet weather, crowded into the houses, the twins along with them. Katanga was telling them stories when Damor called at the door. The room was much too crowded for him to fit in, but he put his head in and said quietly, "Lyn and Greg, did you really mean you would help us if we needed you?"

"Yes," said Greg more boldly than he really felt.

Lyn's throat again grew dry and tight with apprehension, but she managed to say, "Yes, Damor."

He took them aside and said, "Before answering, listen to me, because you will be going into danger, where I cannot protect you. I wish above all things that I did not have to ask you, but many lives are at stake.

"You remember, I am sure, how the little village of Dragon-Cousins behind the palace is surrounded on three sides by a river and on the fourth by the palace. The river is neither broad nor deep, but it is too deep for our Dragon-Cousins to wade through. When the Dark warriors took over the palace, they promptly destroyed the three bridges over this river. Since the Dragon-Cousins cannot pass the palace without being caught by the guard, they are virtual prisoners. As I told you, if we try to rescue them we would be sighted at once; there would be a terrible battle and many dragons and Dragon-Cousins would be slain. You are small and can go through the woods without being seen and you can wade through the river."

"And carry them over?" Greg gasped incredulously. "I don't think that Lyn and I together could even carry *one!*"

"No, you could not, but you can help us build a bridge and also cross over and warn them. Once they are well into the forest, we can meet them at a clearing far enough from the palace so that our wingbeats could not be heard and carry them to safety." He was silent and waited. Greg and Lyn each knew the other was thinking of the happy visit they had made before the King's death to that friendly and gregarious little village. Katanga had taken them there, and for a few hours they had forgotten the gloom that hung over the palace.

"Of course we'll help you. I am glad you asked us," said Greg, firmly shutting his mind to the possible consequences, should they fail.

"And you, Lyn?" Damor said gently.

"Damor, I'm afraid, but I want to help, I do."

Damor touched her gently on the head. "To be afraid and yet to go ahead, that is true bravery."

They followed Damor to where the Captain, several dragons and Dragon-Cousins were gathered. "We have been waiting anxiously for this thick weather, which comes at this time of the year," Damor explained to them. "Each day it delayed, added to our anxiety. Now we must act quickly, for we have sad news about the captives. Tell them," he commanded a Dragon-Cousin.

"The day the Dark villains took the palace, two of us were across the river and heard the bridges being destroyed. We hid and watched. Later in the day I saw my sister who came to draw water, and she agreed to come back each night at a certain time and tell us what was happening to them.

"From the first day they have been treated harshly. Being forced to work long hours with little sleep and food is not the worst of the treatment they are receiving. If their work is not done quickly enough to please their captors, they are struck or burnt with flame. Once, to amuse themselves, the Dark ones took two of our small children, flew up with them, and threw them back and forth as in a game of ball, while their parents watched helplessly below. The dragons laughed at the children's screams and then dropped them. My companion has remained to keep watch and I made my way with all the haste I could to the Mount and found Parte-megan."

"Partemegan signaled to us," Damor took up the account, "and the warriors brought this brave friend here. He and his companion have been stout-hearted, as are all our Dragon-Cousins," (with nods of the head to the Dragon-Cousins present.) "Now, under cover of this heavy mist which all dragons hate to fly in, we shall attempt a rescue."

"How are you going to do it?" Greg asked. His fear was gone and his hatred of the Dark Dragons was growing every minute.

"You and several Dragon-Cousins will build a new bridge while the dragons are feasting as they do each night, gluttons that they are."

"Won't some of the Dragon-Cousins be serving?" Lyn asked.

"Yes, six of them," said the Dragon-Cousin. "But they will be told of the plan. As soon as the serving is finished they have to wash the dishes while the treacherous and villainous Anaconth . . ."

"That is the one you call the assistant cook," Damor interjected.

". . . and his wife themselves are feasting – in one of the royal rooms, no less – while their friends and relations, and even brother and sister, go hungry. At that time the six who serve can follow over the new bridge."

The children discovered that all the preparations had been made and were secretly gratified that Damor had been so confident of their willingness to help. They were also proud to be able to do something important which the powerful dragons could not. Two human beings can feel very useless in a land of warring dragons.

Overriding the Captain's strong objections, Damor insisted on carrying them himself. Four of the best warriors accompanied them. In the heavy fog he seemed to be flying blind and they wondered how he knew where he was going. Dragons, however, have an excellent sense of direction. He landed unhesitatingly in a clearing where several exceptionally large and strong Dragon-Cousins were waiting for them with three long logs, each a good foot wide.

"More dragons will come one by one with carrying nets and will hide in the forest until needed," Damor said. "If all came together the beat of so many wings might be heard and suspicion aroused."

Two loops of vines had been fastened around one end of each log. A dragon lifted that end and a Dragon-Cousin crawled under and slipped a foreleg into each loop. With the log thus resting securely along his back, he crawled laboriously down a path. The twins walked behind this slow cortège until it reached a place where several paths intersected. Here they halted, and Greg was called forward as had been planned.

"You cannot miss the way now," the leading Dragon-Cousin said. "This path goes straight to the river. Cross over at that point; it is less deep there."

Greg ran as fast as he dared through the thick fog with one arm in front of his face in case there should be a low-hanging branch. Fortunately for him, the dragons also used the path occasionally, so Greg had plenty of headroom. The damp loneliness of the foggy path weighed upon him and his thoughts were troubled. He began to wonder if for each person to be free to do exactly as they wanted, was really the best thing. Or did it, as he had heard the Master say, in the end lead to one person wanting his way so much that he would use any means he could to force it upon others? He would ask Damor or Katanga, not the Master, or rather he would not *ask* them, instead he would argue his teacher's points with them. They had once sounded so plausible, so new . . . now he began to suspect they were to be feared.

He came to the river and cautiously stepped into it, afraid each moment that he might trip over a loose stone and fall with a splash. To his relief, the bottom was hard, flat stones and the water was not up to his waist. Turn left, he reminded himself as he reached the opposite bank, then at the ruined bridge go up the path, the head Elder's house will be the second on the right. It was a large house and easy to find. Greg crept up to the low door, knelt down and knocked gently but urgently. In a moment the door opened slightly and a voice said, "Who is there?"

"It is I, Greg. I come from King Damor," he whispered. The door was opened all the way and he crawled in on all fours. In the center room was the Elder who recognized him immediately.

He listened intently as Greg explained Damor's plan, then said with satisfaction to his family, "Did I not say Damor would not fail us?" He promptly ordered one of his sons to go in one direction and a daughter in another to each house and tell the families to go to the river without delaying a moment.

"What about those who are serving the dragons' dinner?" Greg asked, afraid they would be forgotten.

"My wife will go the kitchen and ask for the leftover food as she regularly does – that is all they give us – and will warn the servers to follow as soon as they can."

"There are nineteen families, aren't there?"

The Elder's expression grew sorrowful. "There were until this morning when a husband tried to shield his wife from an angry dragon's flame. This infuriated the dragon and he slew them both, as examples to us," he said. "There are the orphans," he added, indicating two youngsters who were being comforted by the Elder's wife.

Greg went back to the river. After what seemed an interminable wait, though it was really not more than ten minutes, Lyn appeared out of the fog on the other bank. "They are right behind me," she said.

The first Dragon-Cousin appeared and went up to the water's edge, slipped out of his harness, got behind the log and began to push it across. Greg and Lyn each grabbed hold of a loop and hauled and guided the log until it rested securely on the opposite bank. All the logs were quickly in place. Both ends of the new bridge were made level by having stones pushed under them and then the logs were roped together with vines so they would not roll apart.

By the time it was ready, the Elder and his wife had crawled up and stationed themselves one on each side of the bridge. Greg urged them to cross over. The Elder replied, "We are old. It doesn't matter what happens to us. We shall keep count and so be certain none are left behind."

The first to cross was a mother with a basket on her back from which came little whimpers. Lyn, who had visions of the basket sliding into the water, took the basket saying, "Let me carry that," and waded over with it. The mother with a grateful thank-you hurried across. At the next one Greg gave a gasp and Lyn a horrified sob. It was a mother with a young one clinging to her back, a back across which there were terrible burns. Greg lifted the child off and placed it safely on the other side while the mother limped across. Back and forth the twins went. If a child was clinging to a parent's back and seemed too heavy to risk lifting, Greg steadied it from one side and Lyn from the other.

As Lyn placed one child down, she saw the sturdy log carriers were loading themselves up with children who might be too small to keep up. One of them was urging the terribly burnt mother to climb on his back. "Take the children first," she said.

"Lady," said the tough carrier gruffly, "children need their mothers. Climb on." She did so and lay with eyes closed as her carrier disappeared into the fog.

"There must be more than eighteen families," Lyn panted as she kept one ear cocked for the sound of alarm cries, and the line went on and on.

At last the old couple crossed the bridge. "Only those serving remain," the Elder said. With a deep sigh of relief, Greg and Lyn waded once more to the further shore. Ahead of them, the last of the long line were making their slow way down the path.

"Look, Lyn. We can hurry things up by carrying the children. Take the smallest ones first," Greg said. They went along the line gathering up the baskets – there were four of them – from the parents' backs and hurried ahead.

"Tell the dragons to keep them warm," an anxious mother called after them.

Damor was waiting. Six dragonesses had flown in. "They are noted for their quiet flying," he said.

Lyn delivered the mother's message. "Tell the

mothers not to worry," said a dragoness, gathering the baskets together. "I will keep them warm," and she blew warm breaths all around them.

Again and again the twins went back and forth lifting a child from a parent's back and, after placing them over their own shoulders, trotted back to the waiting dragons. Each time the distance was shorter. At last the head of the line reached the clearing, and Damor quickly began sorting them. The strongest ones he sent down another path where further on more dragons waited.

On the six dragonesses who all had carrying pads, he placed the oldest and most badly injured and the dragonesses flew off with the faintest beat of wings. They were back quickly. Damor whispered that they had only carried their burden to another clearing well out of sound of the palace where still other dragons waited. On their last flight they bundled the remaining children into a closely woven carrying net, with the largest on the bottom and the smaller piled on top. As they vanished Damor said, "We must go now; get on my back."

"What about the six who had to stay behind serving?" Lyn asked. "And where is Greg?" she added, looking around in alarm.

"Here I am," he called in a low voice, running up the path. "I went back to see if the six were safe. They are halfway up the path already."

"But that is still a long way for them to go," Lyn objected. "When will their escape be discovered?"

"When the dishes are found unwashed," said a Dragon-Cousin with a grim chuckle. "Do not worry. They know these woods well. It will be easy for the few of them to disappear into the underbrush, and food is plentiful at this time of year."

Greg and Lyn scrambled onto Damor's back and he took off as quietly as he could, but in comparison with the dragonesses he sounded noisy. Out from the trees rose the shape of their warrior escort. They had remained so silent in their hiding places that Lyn had forgotten about them and nearly screamed with fright.

The fog was lightening a little, but twilight was coming down and the visibility was as poor as when they had landed. The dragons flew slowly and carefully. Suddenly Damor swung his head and listened intently. "I think there was a warning cry from the palace." He flew a few wingbeats further, then dropped almost to the treetops and hovered over a clearing and softly called down a warning.

"That is the second place where the dragons are waiting," he whispered, turning his head so that the children could hear him. Confused cries could be heard far behind them. Damor rose higher and higher. Never had he taken them so high.

"Where are you going?" Lyn said as the cooler air flowed around them and the mist lightened until they were just below its uppermost layer.

"Be quiet," Damor said, turning his head and speaking very softly. "Sound travels far in a mist. They will first fly low, scouring the paths and clearings before they rise as high as we are, and by then we shall be out of their reach."

He flew steadily and soon rose until the mist lay below them and a canopy of stars was above them. When he circled down and landed unerringly at the exact place where they had taken off, Lyn drew a deep breath. Never, never would she forget the beauty of that flight under the stars, far above land, where the only sound was the beat of the dragon's great wings.

Damor and his warriors left them and were off again. It was a long time before he returned, but no one wanted to go to bed without hearing if all the Dragon-Cousins had escaped. At every sound of a dragon landing, all conversation stopped, but no newcomer could give them any news. Towards midnight Damor and the warriors at last dropped down weary and hungry. Everyone crowded around them.

"All have been carried to safety except for those who were serving, and they are undoubtedly hiding somewhere," said Damor wearily.

"And now," he said as he finished the food that had been kept hot for them, "I am going to sleep." And so he was, before the dishes were cleared away.

Two days later, Partemegan's bush was waving vigorously and the dragons carried the last captives to the safety of their own land.

CHAPTER 7
A Sign of Hope

"Damor," said Greg, the first thing the next morning, "are you going to try to rescue Edrina now that the Dragon-Cousins have been evacuated?"

The King sighed deeply. "No, the Dragon-Cousins told me much about her. The King's latest 'wife' is furiously jealous. She also desires to lay hold of the jewels which no one can find. No one suspects the Nurse of knowing where they are. All the blame for their loss is laid on you two. This wife tried to take Edrina's collar from her neck and was struck by the King for annoying her. The Nurse who has some freedom told all this to a Dragon-Cousin. There is yet another reason for our not pressing battle. There are several Green Dragons, mostly young ones, who have been taken in by Magior's and Wondan's teachings and look for a new freedom under the Dark King. None of them would, I think, do anything treacherous; they have not strayed that far from the laws of the Great One, at least not yet. None have thrown away their armband, as has Magior, and some are indignant at the Dark King's treatment of their Princess whom they love. She hopes the sight of her imprisonment will move their hearts to turn back before it is too late."

"What of Magior?" asked Lyn.

"He is there all the time."

"Why did he turn traitor?" Lyn could not understand how any Green Dragon could become so treacherous.

"Greed for power, and at the end, anger at my father for having finally seen through his plotting. At first, he probably sought only to gain control over the King and so be able to satisfy his ambition for power. For this reason he practically forced his sister, whom he had always dominated, into marrying my father. The birth of my little Dar-brother opened new possibilities to him, should the King die and he be able to get the little Prince declared King, and the Queen regent. He may even have thought of marrying my sister. Wondan, however, wished to do that also, and Magior may have promised Edrina to Wondan in return for the friendship of the Dark King; for Wondan, as he truly said that day, had great influence with the King. I was to die as well.

"Indeed, I thought nothing of it at the time, but this past winter I was to fly on a certain day to one of the garrisons with two friends. Before we left, my father unexpectedly called for me, and my friends went on without me. They were ambushed and one was slain. It was the old Master who guessed there had been a plot against my life and warned me to be wary where I went and to whom I told my plans. Then I remembered that Magior had been surprised and annoyed to find me with my father that day. But still, I found it hard to believe that one who wore the armband would contemplate such treachery."

"Greed for power feeds on itself," said the Master, who was present, "until it at length becomes

132

insatiable. Only those can hold power safely, who fear its hold on them and who truly follow the laws of the Great One. Remember that, Damor, King of the Green Dragons." Damor promised earnestly he would.

"I can't imagine Damor wanting more and more power," Greg said after the King left.

"Nor can I," said Lyn. "He comes so often to you, Master, for advice on how to be a good King."

"And turns his thoughts frequently to the Blue Road," added the Master.

Greg longed to make some comments, but he did not dare try out his former teacher's ideas on the Master, though he had on Katanga. Katanga had laughed, and in a few words had made the ideas sound stupid. This irked Greg. If the Master had done it, he would not have minded so much. He was an official teacher, but Katanga could claim no such distinction. Greg next tried his arguments on a young warrior. A warrior, he felt confident, would not be learned. This dragon, Tormagon was his name, was young – only sixty – and yet an out-standing warrior who flew with a bit of a swagger. The young dragons and dragonesses admired him tremendously and crowded around him each time he came to the home base. "Stupid of them to do that," Greg said one day when feeling disagreeable.

"Like buying every available picture of favorite soccer players," Lyn retorted, which silenced him. The walls of his room at home were covered with such pictures.

Greg was confident he could out-argue any young warrior and waited for a favorable opportunity when Tormagon was next surrounded by admiring youngsters. Greg was pleased they would hear him, and also pleased that the Master happened to be close by and very likely would also hear. This time he approached the subject cautiously. He did not want to be again classed with the Dark Dragons, but he felt there must be some sort of in-between position of independent thinking and freedom.

"Don't you think everyone should make their own decisions?" he asked.

The warrior looked at him in surprise. "Why, of course," he said, then asked curiously, "do not people in your own place, Earth, make their own decisions, at least once they are grown?"

"Yes, and that means that each one can decide whether they believe in the Great One or not."

The dragon looked at him in complete astonishment. "How can a truth be true or not true according to one's wishes?" He added suspiciously, "Are there Dark Dragons in your place?"

Greg turned red partly from embarrassment, partly from annoyance at having been worsted by an ordinary warrior, and partly from the increasing realization that Tormagon might be right, and there was no halfway. One's thinking had to be either that of the Green Dragons or of the Dark ones.

"To think that a mere warrior is able to answer like that," he muttered to himself, not realizing the Master had approached him. "Probably he just learned everything by rote."

"Do not be deceived by Tormagon's youth. His heart is true, and in admiring him, the youngsters will strengthen their love of what is good and true."

After much consultation with the Master, his Councillors and the Captain, Damor reluctantly decided to move his headquarters further back of the patrolled line to a more central location. He still slept at night with the warriors but spent most of his time with his people and the Dragon-Cousins.

"Shouldn't a Dragon King's first place be with his warriors?" Greg asked Katanga, surprised at Damor's move. "That is how it always seems to be in the tales we hear. And that is where he wants to be."

"Of course he wants to be with the warriors. That is the way it should be. But there are plenty of warriors, some more able than the King will ever be, so says the Captain privately, though he is quick to add that the King is a good warrior. Our urgent need at this moment is for a great ruler, and I am certain that my beloved King can be that. Have you not noticed how he never thinks of himself, and spends himself tirelessly listening to and encouraging those who come to him, and flying from place to place to speak with those who cannot or do not come? Can you not feel the difference that has already come upon the kingdom? Everyone has been half neglected for so long, and now all are pleased that the King thinks of them and takes interest in their affairs. Little by little he is weaving the web of a strong, united kingdom. He may never be the mighty warrior that Nimeon the Great was, but I think he will be as great a ruler as Nimeon who loved his people and was beloved by them."

One day Damor went to see the Queen and took

the twins with him. "She is with her parents," he told them.

The Queen was lying in the warm sun. Beside her, curled up, fast asleep, was a plump baby dragon. She greeted Damor and the children warmly and appeared more cheerful than they had ever seen her. Lyn bent over the baby to see him better. He woke up with a squeal of fright at the sight of this queer stranger and darted under the Queen's wing, leaving only the tip of his tail sticking out.

"He has never seen anything like you," said the Queen with a placid chuckle. The Queen caught Lyn's questioning glance. "That is the little one who was shown to the Gathering," she explained.

"Were you the one who came back for him?" Lyn asked.

"Yes, I feared he would be forgotten and felt I would be to blame if anything happened to him. So far his parents have not been found. Alas! The mother may have been slain for the sake of her son; so I shall be a mother to him." The baby had cautiously poked his nose out and was watching the strangers. "See how lively and healthy he is," she said contentedly.

Before leaving, Damor spoke privately with her.

"I asked her about my father's death," he said when they were in flight again. "She said she was in the next room and heard her brother talking to my father, and my father answering him angrily. Then my father cried out that he had been poisoned. Magior laughed and said, 'You thought you could send me away, did you? This is my revenge, and

136

Damor shall follow you!' She called for Orimalgon who had already heard the King's cry. He was entering and probably heard Magior's words. Magior must have guessed it, and that is why he slew him."

"So Magior *did* kill your father."

"Magior or Anaconth; we may never know which. She also told me," Damor continued, "that Magior had originally only intended to use the substitute baby at the Gathering as the sickly little Prince was showing signs of another cold. Then, when the Prince went Home, he would not be swerved from his plan though the Queen pleaded with him. He threatened her with imprisonment if she did not come with him to the Gathering. She went out of fear. It was the Old Master's words that gave her the courage to speak the truth."

"Could Magior really have succeeded in pretending that baby was the Prince?" Lyn asked.

"Had the Queen consented, he might have. Few ever saw the child. His markings were still blurred, and only those who knew him well – and Magior would have seen to it that none of them came near him – could have told him from another whose markings were similar."

There were two hatching nurseries in the southern area. Each time Damor was near one, he would stop and speak to the nurse and guards, and ask how many babies had been born and to whom, and were they healthy. "They are our future," he said. "I fear there will be many widows and orphans before we win back our land," he added with a sigh.

"Well, you are doing your best to prevent it," said Greg. He had wondered why Damor and the

Captain made so few sorties. Every now and then, the Dark Dragons attacked and then there was a fierce fight, but that was infrequent.

"They have many good warriors and their King is one of the fiercest and most skillful." Greg remembered with a shudder the huge black and gray form on the Mount with the terrible scar like a double "S" on his chest and cruel black eyes, so different from Damor's green and gold ones. "This is our land," Damor continued, "and we shall regain it, but if we are wise and skillful we may keep our losses low."

Greg and Lyn wondered privately how the dragons were going to do it until they noticed that the lines of patrol were much farther away than before.

"Yes, little by little we are pushing the line upwards while warriors in the north push downwards. The Dark King is at a disadvantage for he has to guard both what he has taken from us and his own land, or else we shall invade it as we are already doing in the south. We are not trying to conquer his land but are raiding his flocks and stores. He has had to send warriors there, which weakens his force here. Next we shall raid in the north and force him to remove more of his warriors. I have given orders for my warriors to avoid a heavy battle so there will be little fighting, but he will not dare withdraw his forces from the north and south."

"Then you will make a final push in the center and drive them out," said Greg triumphantly.

"Yes," said Damor and sighed heavily again. "I still hope the young ones will return before that happens . . . and there is Edrina."

They were flying near one of the nurseries one day when Damor swerved and started circling down rapidly.

"What's the matter?" Lyn asked.

"Something has happened at that nursery. I fear there may have been an accident."

They looked down. There was an unusual commotion. Several dragons had gathered at the edge, including the guards, and the nurse was waving her head excitedly.

"Sire!" she cried when she saw the King. "Look!"

Damor landed swiftly. The children jumped off and ran over to look. A pair of dragons was busily drying off their newborn son. The baby was purple!

"At last!" cried Damor joyfully. "The line of Masters will not be broken!"

Everyone present was rejoicing and congratulating the parents. It was their third child, they told the King. The father, a messenger dragon, was more excited than his wife. "Time enough for rejoicing afterwards," she said, "but he has to be dried off now," and she continued to do it vigorously.

She did pause for a few moments out of respect for the Master when he arrived after hearing the news. Lyn's eyes filled with tears as she watched the Master lean over and gently touch the head of his small successor. She rejoiced with the Green Dragons. "They are doing their best to be faithful," she said to Greg, "and a new Master has been given them."

By evening the news had spread among the dragons and Dragon-Cousins. She could sense a complete change. They had new hope. The sign they had longed for had come. The talk was all about the "Little Master".

"Is that what he will be called?" Greg asked Damor.

"No, he will be called by whatever name his parents give him until he takes his place as the Master's assistant."

"When will that be?"

"I do not know. He will eat and sleep and play and grow and be taught like all the other little ones. Then one day, probably when he comes of age, he will bid farewell to his parents and take his place on the Mount with the Master. He alone will know when to go."

Though Lyn and Greg enjoyed talking with any of the dragons and Dragon-Cousins, they preferred to be with Damor or Katanga. Lyn also loved to be with the Master, though, as she confided to Greg, "His silences are longer than anyone else's."

Greg, on the contrary, kept away from the Master as much as he could without it appearing obvious. His mind was greatly troubled. He no longer wanted any of the Dark Dragons' ideas or philosophy; on the contrary, now he detested all they stood for, but he had so often and so tenaciously held forth on certain "progressive" ideas, as his former teacher called them, that he could not keep them from returning to his mind. At moments when he was the happiest and most greatly admiring his new friends, these dark thoughts would come back to torment him. Who was right and who was wrong?

Damor and Katanga to whom he partly confided

his doubts had the same answer, "Speak to the Master." But Greg could not get up courage to do that. What would the Master think of him? Suppose he counseled Damor to send him back through the Door, or, when his spirits were at their lowest, perhaps even tell him, as Lyn once had, that his place was with the Dark Dragons? Lyn would understand, he was sure, but he did not dare confide in her. She was so happy and contented; suppose he filled her with his doubts? That she had resisted his vigorous attempts to do so ever since the beginning of the summer did not reassure him. Lyn, however, knew her twin too well not to sense something was wrong. Her solution was the same as Damor's and Katanga's: he must speak with the Master, and she watched for an opportunity to get him to do so.

It came one hot afternoon. She ran over to Greg. "Remember the mischievous little dragons having their first lesson on the Mount? Come and see how quickly the older ones learn to behave."

A group of half-grown youngsters this time were listening silently and intently to the Master. But it was not that which caught Greg's attention, but rather the way the Master taught. He waited until the lesson was over and then asked curiously, "The laws you teach them all seem to be 'Do's', ours are mostly 'Don'ts'."

"What do you mean?"

Greg thought wildly for an example. Traffic laws would mean nothing to them, nor school rules, nor . . . In desperation he recited the Ten Commandments. "You see, they are mostly 'Don'ts.' "

The Master listened gravely. "They are all good

and true," he said, "but they are only the beginning, the foundation upon which the rest must be built."

"What do you mean?" said Greg in bewilderment.

"Take, for instance, *'Do not steal.'* Of course, no one must steal. The very young who have not yet learned to think, have to be taught not to take their playmate's ball or his food, if necessary with the help of gentle punishment. But their learning cannot end there. They may never steal, but the wanting of what is another's would remain. They must be taught little by little, starting as soon as they can understand, that happiness comes not from taking but from giving and sharing and – when their hearts and thoughts are fully grown – to be happy in the pleasure of others. Then they will never even desire to have what is not theirs. Do you understand?"

"I think so," said Greg, wondering if human beings could ever change their thinking so much. If only we could, he found himself thinking, there would never be another war. "What about the other Commandments?"

The Master chuckled. "What I have said would give a dragon enough to think about for a long time. They would ponder it over and over again as they grew older and each time their thoughts would become wider and deeper." He fell silent.

As they walked away Greg said ruefully to Lyn, "He might just as well have said, 'Go and do likewise.' "

Greg did not mention this conversation again, but Lyn saw him later in earnest conversation with the Master. He came away from the interview looking happier than Lyn had seen him look for months and was noticeably less pugnacious. He did not change all at once, and could still be overbearing, but he *was* changing, and she could see that though he still argued, it was more and more for fun, and he laughed when bested in an argument instead of being annoyed.

They made many friends among the dragons who lived within walking distance, and when not with Damor or Katanga or needed to give a helping hand, they would visit. One of those whom they particularly enjoyed visiting was a young mother who was chattier than most dragons. They would sit talking together on the grass in front of her house while her only child, an exceptionally active little dragon of three passings, romped joyously on the grass with his favorite toy, a bright red ball.

To their dismay, one afternoon when they walked over, no happy little dragon dashed out to greet them. Instead they saw Katanga with his basket of remedies and a sorrowful father who was listening to the Master saying, "There is nothing more we can do to help. The sickness must run its course. Now I am needed elsewhere."

"What is wrong?" Greg asked Katanga.

"Their little son has caught a bad chest cold, no one knows how, as it is not the weather for colds. He is very ill and will go Home soon, I think, as his little fire has nearly gone out."

"Isn't there *anything* more you can do?" asked Lyn.

Katanga shook his head.

Greg, more to break the sad silence than any-

143

thing else, said, "Have you tried everything? What about a mustard plaster?"

"A mustard plaster? What is that?"

"It is something we put on our chests. I used to have bad chest colds when I was small and my grandmother made them for me. She said they were very old-fashioned, but they worked."

"How is it made?"

"You take mustard. I don't know what you call it here, but there was plenty in the roast last night; it nearly burnt my mouth."

"Mine too," interjected Lyn.

"Then it is made into a paste with water and put on a cloth which is put on the chest."

"A wet paste on a baby's chest!" exclaimed Katanga incredulously.

"Oh, a warm flannel is put on top. But don't worry, the paste really gets you hot. The mustard makes a wet heat that penetrates the chest and helps break up the congestion. At least I think that is how it works. There is nothing like it. By the next morning I would be fine."

"Wait," Katanga called to the Master who was spreading his wings to leave. He scuttled over and repeated to the Master what Greg had just said. The Master questioned Greg closely about the mustard plaster.

"I don't know if it would work on a baby dragon, and I don't want to suggest anything that might harm him," said Greg miserably. "After all, you are the Master of Wisdom and know far more about such things than I do."

"It is poor wisdom not to know that new knowledge may lurk anywhere and may be lost forever if one is not willing to admit it may be there. Many who think themselves wise are not, because they look for wisdom only where they expect to find it, and therefore much passes them by." He turned to the dragon father. "Do you wish this new remedy to be tried?"

The father was silent for a moment, then said quietly, "Master, it is not I who have knowledge in such matters, but you."

"The consent must come from you and your wife. But my advice is that you let it be tried, for unless this remedy works, your little son will undoubtedly go Home before morning."

The mother who was crouched by the crib weeping and trying to keep the baby warm by softly blowing on him agreed at once.

"I think by mustard you mean the herb matil," said Katanga. "Is there any in your kitchen?" he asked the mother.

The dragoness quickly showed him where it was. Greg tasted it. "This is it," he said, screwing up his face. "It tastes just like mustard."

On the same shelf was a rounded rock used by the dragons for crushing various tough stalks. It was so large Greg needed both hands to use it to mash enough of the matil.

"Let me have your scarf, Lyn," he said. "It's bigger than my handkerchief and much cleaner."

He took the wet mash over to the crib. The baby was lying with his bright red ball unheeded beside him. He was breathing with difficulty and choked every now and then. His small inner fire was indeed close to being extinguished.

Greg spread the plaster on the scarf and doubled it over. He took off the soft rabbit-type skin that was already tied over the child's chest. "Warm that," he said to the mother. He put the scarf on the baby's small chest and tied it around its neck. He then placed the warmed skin on top of the scarf.

"I don't know how much matil to use on a baby dragon," he said worriedly to Katanga. "Too much might blister his skin, and too little would not do much good. We'll have to watch it carefully." Katanga nodded and with that nod, Greg suddenly felt one with the Healers, with all healers. With his Uncle Jack, too.

"You go back, Lyn," Greg suggested. It was nearly nightfall. She did. She knew there was nothing she could do and would be in the way if she remained, and she didn't want to be there if that happy little baby went Home.

Greg and Katanga watched and waited all through the long night. While the parents stayed by the crib, they sat on the grass by the door. Every now and then one or the other would creep in and look at the baby who, to Greg's eyes, looked no better. As he waited, over and over again the thought came to him of his Uncle Jack waiting and watching and trying to save some sick child in that far-off place, Earth.

Towards morning without meaning to, he fell asleep, tired out with watching. Sunrise woke him. He jumped up and looked through the doorway. Katanga and the parents were by the crib. The mother was weeping. Sick at heart, Greg forced him self to go in and look. That's what a good doctor would do, he told himself. The baby was stretching sleepily; its breathing was perfectly normal, and in another moment he gave a hungry wail. The parents leaned over and caressed him, weeping so much with happiness that Greg felt he was caught in a warm shower.

The next day the baby was out in the sunshine sitting on his haunches in his crib with his little head peering over the edge. And on the next he was on the lawn again playing with his red ball as though he had never been ill.

After that, many babies were saved by means of hot mustard plasters and Greg was considered a remarkable Healer.

"But I don't feel like one at all," he said to Lyn. "Grandma was the healer. All I can think of is how often I thought her remedies silly and out-of-date."

CHAPTER 8
A Hidden Menace

What Katanga had said about Damor was true. Back and forth, up and down he went, speaking with everyone, young and old, ending small quarrels (there were few of these) with kind words, and listening to questions or, with the old, to their tales and advice for hours at a time. Or he would just be silent with them, which among dragons is a sign of real friendship. He was a great favorite with the young. He rolled balls for the very small while talking with their parents, played with the somewhat older children and encouraged the almost-grown in their hopes. He was in great demand for ball games by the young and full-grown alike. This is rather like an air-borne game of volleyball played with a large ball but without a net. The "courts" are "marked out" by landmarks below. It is a lively game that demands great wingskill and is popular with both dragons and dragonesses. The King excelled at the game which increased his popularity.

Nor did Damor feign this interest. He loved his people, and they knew it. He was determined to give them the leadership which they both wanted and needed, and which he alone as King could give them. So little by little, as Katanga had foretold, the bonds between the King and every dragon in the realm were first forged and then strengthened.

The Master, too, went tirelessly back and forth,

148

teaching, encouraging, healing. "He will be one of the wisest of our many wise Masters," said Katanga. "See how many are coming to consult him or just to receive comfort from his words and wisdom. And that is how it should be."

Wherever he went, Damor usually took Greg and Lyn with him to their great delight. When he talked and listened they tried to be helpful which pleased the dragons and Dragon-Cousins immensely. Gathering dead branches for the fires needed for cooking was their most frequent occupation. Being more agile than the Dragon-Cousins or even the young dragons, they were able to pile firewood in half the time the others could.

Around a small, pretty, blue lake where pink herons fished undisturbed among its reeds at one end and a colony of frogs sat (with one eye on the herons) on lily pads at the other end, were several tree-dotted fields that were a favorite meeting place of the dragons. The children played in and above the field while their mothers watched, the elderly lay under the trees and exchanged tales, and the more active dragons enjoyed themselves in other sports. For this reason both Damor and the Master often went there. Besides, a little way beyond the fields was the house where the Little Master's parents lived.

"I think you come here as much to see the Little Master as to speak with the dragons," Lyn said teasingly to Damor one day.

He laughed. "You are right. I do come here partly to see him and to rejoice in him. We all do. Have you not noticed how often the warriors on home-leave stop by to look at him? The sight of him strengthens us."

The Little Master was usually to be found in a sunny, very low-walled enclosure with several other babies and a dragoness who watched over them.

"The mothers of the babies take turns looking after them," the children were told. "Normally each baby stays with its mother; but with so many more dragons than usual in the area, and more coming to see him, there would be danger of their being hurt. At night they go home to their mothers."

A deep forest of huge trees came right up to this group of houses in the back and half circled them. Here the twins worked hard collecting firewood. All the dead branches had been gathered up long ago and so when needed, a tree was cut down. This was fun to watch. A half-dead tree that was going to fall soon was chosen; there were plenty of them. First a dragon cut off the lower branches with spurts of flame as high as he could reach. Then, working from one side of the trunk and then from the other, he would blow a thin spout of flame by pursing his lips. The dragons' control of the shape and intensity of their flame was amazing. At the last moment he would give a cry of warning to those around, and down came the tree. If the dragon was expert the tree fell exactly where he wanted it to. The cutting of the branches into useful lengths was left to the younger dragons who divided into teams and made a game of it. This firewood was left lying to be collected as needed.

At Greg's suggestion several large carrying baskets were placed near the fallen tree. These he and

Lyn filled. Afterwards, Dragon-Cousins, whose backs are immensely strong, carried them to a central location.

One hot day, Damor arrived at this lake area with Greg and Lyn, to find the Master already there tending to two children who had collided in mid-air during a ball game. A new tree had been cut down, so Lyn and Greg climbed the slope from the field to the forest, stopping for a moment to watch the Little Master and to chat with the nurse. The tree was a big one and they worked hard for a long time picking up the branches. When at last the baskets were filled and the remaining branches piled beside them, they were hot and tired and sat down with their backs against a mammoth tree trunk to rest. They did not talk. Lyn was trying to suck a splinter out of her finger and Greg was struggling with a particularly hard knot in his shoelace. Behind them they heard voices, Dragon-Cousins' voices which, being higher pitched, were easily distinguishable from those of the dragons. At first, neither of them paid much attention, thinking they were coming for the baskets. Greg was about to get up to help load the baskets onto their backs when he caught the words, "Don't forget to put on your armband. You could not get near him without it."

A voice answered, "I will, just before I reach the houses. Since I took it off, it has become so loose that it slips down and that would be noticed, too."

Greg caught Lyn's arm and pulled her down beside him in the long grass. The first voice said, "Follow that path to the houses. You can skirt around them if necessary. I am going back now, as I am too well known here. Give me time to get away so there is no chance of our being seen together."

There came the sound of a Dragon-Cousin shuffling off, and shortly after, the second one left. As he crawled away, Greg peered around the trunk of the tree and then stood up to see the markings. His heart nearly stopped: it was the assistant cook.

As soon as he was out of sight, Greg whispered the news to Lyn.

"We've got to trail them," she said. "You take one, and I'll take the other."

"No, it's more important for Damor to know what is happening. The cook's the real villain. Let's see what he's up to first and then warn Damor. We'll go up the other path to the houses. That's a short cut."

They ran up the shorter path and hid behind the tree on the edge of the forest from where they could see the path the cook had taken. In a few minutes the Dragon-Cousin appeared. Greg had not been mistaken. It was the assistant cook. No one was around, and he headed straight for the houses.

"Duck through that forest and get Damor as fast as you can," Greg ordered his sister. She ran back through the trees, came out beyond the other path, and tore down the hill toward the field where they had left the King.

Hugging the walls of the houses so as not to be seen, Greg followed the assistant cook until he saw him heading toward the babies' enclosure. Alarmed, he hurried up behind as quietly as he could. The Dragon-Cousin was looking casually over the low wall as so many did, and Greg, peering out from behind a tree that shaded the enclosure, saw him eyeing the nurse every now and then. She was at the other end chatting with another dragoness. At a moment when her head was turned away, the cook lifted himself half over the wall, quickly threw something in front of the purple baby, and then hurried off, but not so fast as to be suspected of running away. The little one crawled towards the object with its mouth open. In a flash Greg realized what was happening. Yelling "Poison!", he threw himself over the wall and got his hand on the morsel just as the little dragon's jaw closed on it. The baby sank its sharp teeth into Greg's hand and held on with bulldog tenacity. But Greg's yell had brought instant results. The nurse took in the situation with a glance, swung her head with a lightening movement and caught the baby up by his tail. She held him head downward so that he could not possibly swallow. The baby opened its mouth in unbelievably loud wails, letting go of Greg's hand as he did so. The other dragoness with a swift movement of her wings leapt into the air and landed on the Dragon-Cousin just as he was reaching the cover of the forest. She held him down, calling loudly for help, while he struggled and bit at her.

Mothers shot out of the houses. Warriors dropped down as if by magic – they had been playing ball overhead – and the words "poisoning the Little Master" were passed from dragon to dragon.

"Do not let any of the other babies get near the place where the poison was," said the nurse, who was holding the Little Master's mouth wide open and vigorously cleaning it with her tongue, which

153

temporarily muffled its yells.

Greg promptly sat down on the spot, still clutching the morsel in his bleeding hand. The rest of the babies were running around also, wailing miserably. A mother hopped into the enclosure, scooped them close to her, and glared fiercely around, while other mothers pushed forward, calling loudly for their babies. Into this tumult, Damor dropped like a thunderbolt, with the Master following more slowly.

"Silence!" thundered the King. "What has happened?" he demanded.

As soon as the assistant cook saw the King he began protesting loudly and demanding his release.

"Why are you holding him?" Damor asked the dragoness. She explained what had happened. Greg got up and told Damor about the conversation they had heard in the forest and how he had seen the assistant cook throw something right in front of the Little Master.

Another murmur of anger passed through the group, and the Dragon-Cousin again protested his innocence. "Let me go," he snarled.

Damor ordered two warriors to guard him, and the dragoness reluctantly released him.

"Come here," Damor said to Greg. "Show us what was thrown in." Greg did so, and suddenly felt very foolish – suppose it was all a mistake?

The Master took it and smelled it. "It is gafa," he said gravely, and handed it to a Dragon-Cousin, a local Healer, who had crawled up.

He also smelled it, touched it with his tongue, and said, "Yes, it is gafa."

There was another murmur, this time of anger

and horror. "What is gafa?" Lyn asked a dragoness. She had run back and managed to squeeze herself through the crowd to the front.

"It is used to clean wounds, but it is poison to eat."

"A piece this size would have caused the little one to die in great pain," continued the Master.

The dragons were furious and the guards no longer merely watched the assistant cook, but held him none too gently in their talons.

"I am innocent," he practically snarled. "It was that Earth person who threw the piece in. I was just watching the children play."

Greg noticed the Dragon-Cousin was not looking the King straight in the eyes. The dragons saw it also.

"He is lying!" cried a dragoness.

"You say you saw him put on the gold armband?" the Master questioned Greg.

"I didn't actually see him put it on, but I heard him say it no longer fit since he had taken it off. He was carrying it in his mouth when he left the place where we saw the two of them talking together. My sister also saw it and heard what he said."

"Yes," Lyn, still panting from her run, added her testimony. "I also heard him say that, and saw him with his armband in his mouth."

The Master leaned over and spoke to the King in a voice too low to be heard. Damor sat back on his haunches.

"Take our Dragon-Cousin, Anaconth," he said to the guard, "and shake him." Lyn and Greg watched in bewilderment. With a beat of their wings, the two warriors lifted him above the dragons' heads and shook him vigorously. The gold armband flew off and rolled on the ground.

"Anaconth. By this you are proved a traitor, for never would the armband have come off one who had not taken it off previously by his own choice." Damor's voice became sterner. "Not only did you try to poison the Little Master, but now I accuse you of being an accomplice in my father's death, if not his actual poisoner."

Anaconth started. Evidently he had thought his part in the old King's murder was not even suspected. "I did not do it," he protested volubly. "Magior did. He is the villain. He must have hidden somewhere near the kitchen and poisoned the potion Orimalgon was brewing. I did not know he was there. I had nothing to do with it."

"He was in the storeroom right by the kitchen that night, and you knew it! You came out of that room after I had seen him and assured us no one was there. It isn't as if a dragon could hide in there without you seeing him!" cried Lyn angrily.

"You are also a traitor, Anaconth," continued the King, "not only to the dragons but to your own people, even to your close kinsmen. While they toiled and were half-starved and beaten when held captive, you and your wife feasted and enjoyed the favor of the Dark King. What answer do you make to that charge?"

"Self-defense! We thought if we kept in favor with the King, we would be in a position to help our kindred and even free them," said Anaconth.

"Almost as smoothly as Magior," Greg murmured to Lyn.

"I like that," interpolated a Dragon-Cousin. "I was there. You did nothing of the sort."

"You are proved a triple traitor to the laws of the Great One and the pledge you made when you put on the gold armband. There is no room for traitors among us."

At these words Anaconth threw all pretense to the wind and hurled insults and accusations at the King, Lyn and Greg: "Spies! Liars! Murderers! Scum from another world!"

"Take him away," Damor ordered the guard. The warriors caught him up and flew off. He was never seen again.

The nurse dragoness assured the King that none of the children were harmed, only frightened.

"Where is the mother of the Little Master?" Damor called.

His mother had already pushed her way to the enclosure and taken him from the nurse and his wails were rapidly subsiding.

"Keep a close watch on him," said Damor, "and be very careful of what he eats. Do not let anyone feed him or prepare his food except yourself."

The mother nodded her grateful assent to the King, tucked the now contentedly grunting baby on her back between her wings and went off.

The next day the house where the Little Master lived was empty.

"They have been taken to a safe place," Damor said.

"How did the Dark Dragons know about the Little Master?" Lyn asked.

"Our warriors were imprudent. Such was their rejoicing at his birth they could not forbear answering certain taunts of an enemy patrol who were goading them about having no younger Master. They retorted that they did indeed have one. I suspect the Dark King or else Magior thought up the plan of having Anaconth and his wife act first as spies and then as murderers. Very likely they were only too anxious to do something which would regain their lost favor with the King, who must have blamed them for the escape of the Dragon-Cousins. It would not have been hard for them to slip through the forests under our patrol and then hang around and listen until they discovered where the Little Master lived."

"Did Anaconth's wife get away?"

"No," Damor replied shortly, and then spoke on other matters.

CHAPTER 9
Ralawir

Nothing had come of Damor's hopes of regaining the strayed young dragons until one evening a warrior of the patrol brought one to the King. He was almost full-grown and was ashamed and repentant. His story was soon told. He and a friend had been enticed by Wondan's promises of new freedoms, and what was worse, his younger brother who loved him dearly had followed them. The Dark King's treatment of the Dragon-Cousins and the Princess' imprisonment made him indignant. His folly became clear to him upon the death of his friend. This friend had paid too much attention to one of the Dark King's favorite dragonesses and she to him. "My friend was slain by their King himself," said the young dragon, "and he laughed at the freedoms we had been promised even as he slew him. I would have fled at once, but my younger brother, who is only thirty, had captured the fancy of the King's favorite wife, who flattered and petted him and kept him as her servant. His head was turned and he would not listen to me, but still I could not abandon him.

"Yesterday the Princess' Nurse berated me for my faithlessness. In my anguish I told her everything. She comforted me though I did not deserve it. This afternoon she told me the Princess had pro-

159

cured my brother's freedom. That same Dark Dragoness greatly coveted the Princess' gold collar, and the Princess agreed to give it to her if she freed my brother from her thrall. The dragoness kept her part of the bargain. She turned on my brother and scolded him and beat him and drove him away from her, telling him she was tired of him and would have him slain if she ever set eyes on him again. In his misery and bewilderment he came to me, and we fled together."

"Where is he now?"

"Sire," said the warrior who had brought the repentant dragon, "he was badly bruised from his beating and too weary to fly any farther. He is now at one of our patrol stations."

"Sire, slay me if you will, for I deserve punishment, but have mercy on my brother," pleaded the dragon, "for he went to the Dark ones only because he always looked up to me and imitated all I did." The dragon was weeping. "I failed him."

Damor was silent, then said sternly, "Do you completely forswear the Dark Dragons and their ways and ideas?"

"Sire, I hate the very sight of them."

"Are you willing to do all the Master tells you?"

"With great joy, Sire."

"Then I pardon you and your brother. Go now to the Master, and your brother must do the same as soon as he is rested."

The young dragon choked, then looked straight at the King and said with a quiet intensity that made him sound suddenly much older, "My King, if ever I can prove my gratitude by giving my life for you, I shall rejoice to do so."

"I like him," Lyn whispered to Katanga.

"Yes, he is a true Green Dragon at heart and the Dark ones will never fool him again."

The young dragon was able to give the King much useful information. Not as many Green Dragons as Damor had feared had followed the Dark ones. Three young ones remained. A fourth had fled, probably to the north where his family lived, and another had been slain when attempting to escape. There was a fat and lazy elderly pair who did nothing but eat and sleep all day, though since the Dragon-Cousins' escape they had to wash the dishes, and also a young couple whom he thought were now living in the Dark Dragons' land. He did not know how many Dragon-Cousins other than Anaconth and his wife had gone over to the Dark Dragons. The Dark King, as Damor suspected, had blamed Anaconth and his wife for the Dragon-Cousins' escape and had forced them to work from morning to night. But lately they had not been around.

"What about my sister, the Princess Edrina?"

"So far, Sire, she has been well treated. She is allowed a short flight twice a day, closely guarded, of course. The King presses his suit and wishes to marry her according to our ways so that he can pretend to claim the throne through her.

"She has held him off by telling him of her great scruples at marrying under the age permitted by our laws – saying, 'Suppose, because of this, it were not considered a true marriage,' and much more. Thus far he has tried to overcome her resistance by coax-

161

ings and cajolings, but he is getting impatient."

Damor spent a long time in consultation with the Captain that night. What their plans were was never known because an unexpected happening changed everything.

Since the mustard plaster incident, Greg spent all the extra time he could with Katanga and the other Healers. He learned how to dress a warrior's wound, saw how they made a cast for a broken leg or wing with straight pieces of wood firmly bound to the limb. He was especially interested in certain large leaves that were placed on a fresh wound to prevent it from festering and which hastened the healing. He wondered what their curative powers were. His hands made him adept in pounding the various barks and seed pods that were used in various ointments and potions.

Katanga was noted for his cleverness in finding herbs and barks and a strange, twisted, yellow root which grew only in the deepest forests. He was glad to have Greg for company and the two frequently went off on such excursions. Lyn noticed that Greg came back from these expeditions quieter, more agreeable and with a greater sense of purpose, and that he boasted frequently now to all who would listen about their Healer uncle.

A few nights after the two young dragons' escape, he and Katanga went on an expedition to search for this rare root which was easier to find at night because then its surface leaves gave forth a pungent odor. Damor was at the southern garrison taking part in a raid which he insisted on doing. Lyn was alone with the Master, the Captain and several other dragons. An elderly dragon was in the middle of an exciting story when a warning cry came from a guard. He called down to the Captain that a Dark warrior asked for a safe conduct.

"Terms of surrender, do you think?" Lyn exclaimed excitedly. "Oh, if only this war were over and everyone could go back to their homes!"

"If only it were . . ." said the Master with a sigh.

"Let him pass," called back the Captain, "with a guard."

In a moment two warriors dropped down with a Dark Dragon between them.

"He wishes to speak with our King," explained one of the guards.

"King Damor is not here," said the Captain. "I am the Captain of the Border Guard and next in command. Will you state your errand, or do you wish to wait until the King returns?"

"There is no time to wait," said the Dark warrior, who looked about Tormagon's age.

"Why is there not time?" asked the Captain.

The dragon did not answer. He was staring at the Master and said in a low voice, "Are you the Master?"

The Master looked at him intently. "Yes, I am."

The dragon bowed his dark head, respectfully, it seemed to Lyn, and from then on spoke only to the Master. The Captain repeated his question and the dragon started, as though he had just heard it.

"I wished to speak to your King because I bring news of his sister, the Princess. She is held prisoner."

"We know that," said the Captain, "and that she

refuses to obtain her freedom by marrying your King."

"She has refused once too often."

"What do you mean?" the Captain said in alarm. "She would die before marrying him!"

"I believe she would, for she is a brave Princess. But would she still refuse if forced to watch three of your young ones, children only, being cruelly slain before her when she could free them by accepting him?"

There was a general gasp and wrathful exclamations.

"What has happened?" the Captain growled, twitching his tail with controlled fury. "And why have you been sent to tell us this?"

"I have not been sent," returned the dragon. "I chose freely myself to come and tell you, and none know of my coming."

"Why?"

The dragon was silent for a long time until the Master leaned forward and said quietly to him, "My son, you have had the courage to come to us, can you not find the still greater courage to tell us why?"

"Master, my name is Ralawir. When our King led us to your land, I soon saw that your ways are not like ours. It was also clear to me that much of what I had been told about you was not so. Above all I wondered why our warriors and even our King, who is such a fierce and mighty warrior and fearless in battle, shunned the place you call the Mount and even more what you call the Blue Road. It can be seen in flight, but not clearly, and we have strict orders not to go near the sea except to attack those flying north or south along the shore.

"I was determined to find out what caused such fear and uneasiness. One day when I was off duty I flew to the Mount and landed. Such fear came upon me that, though I was ashamed, I did not at once turn around. At last I did and saw the Blue Road. I do not know how long I stayed, but when I left I both feared and longed to come back and look again."

"And did you?" asked the Master, and his eyes were more like those of the old Master than Lyn had ever seen them before. There was not the slightest sound from the other dragons as they awaited his answer.

"Yes, Master. I went back again and yet again, for I could not bear to stay away. And the more I looked the less grew my fears and the greater my longing to return. Much have I thought these days, or rather perhaps I have learned much; I cannot always tell the difference."

"It is both, my son," said the Master softly.

"My heart is greatly troubled. I am a warrior and I serve my King, but now I do not think he was right to invade this land; and there are things my friends do which I now think wrong.

"Today I heard, for I was present, being on duty, my King threaten the three young ones and tell the Princess she had until tomorrow to decide whether she would marry him. If she still refuses he would force her to go to the courtyard where first the children's wings would be broken and then they would be slowly put to death. The children were in terrible fear, and your Princess, brave though she is, only with great effort kept from weeping. After they were all back under guard, I knew I could never return and look on the Blue Road unless I attempted to save them."

The Captain, who had been watching him closely, nodded approvingly and said under his breath, "He speaks the truth." Aloud he said, "What is your plan?"

"The Princess has been imprisoned with the youngsters in an effort to weaken her will. Tonight I shall be on guard from the middle of the night until dawn at the only door from which they can escape the palace. They are in a room on the passage which leads to a small courtyard. Since the hall is narrow, a dragon on guard in front of the door of that room would block the whole passage. As I said, I shall be at the outer door. Another guard is at the end, but around the corner in the wider hall. Every now and then, he looks down the passage to order them back into the room if they dare to come out. There are also other guards outside the palace, but the only one who can see me at my post is the tower guard. He would give the alarm if he saw them escaping; but it is part of his duties during his watch to fly several times around the palace grounds, which, as you know, are large, in case any enemy attempts to enter the grounds. Our King has not forgotten the escape of the Dragon-Cousins. The Princess' only hope of escape is during the short space of time his flight takes."

"Why do you come to us?" asked the Captain. "Do you wish some of our warriors to be near to

166

protect the Princess once she is free?"

"A little space beyond your patrol lines, yes, but not far or else you will be noticed and our patrol line strengthened. No, I come here because unless the Princess and the others stand ready to flee the moment I give the signal they will not have time, as they must go through the courtyard and be in flight before the guard returns to the tower. If I signal as the guard flies off on his rounds and they make haste, he will very likely be at his farthest point from the tower when they take to the air; he may or may not see them, but that chance they must take. I dare not go down the passage ahead of time to explain to her, nor would there be time before the guard swung back. Yet she must be warned ahead." He paused.

All had their eyes fixed on him.

"I have heard there are among you two strangers from another place, who are smaller than your Dragon-Cousins and yet very agile. If one came with me, I can land on a flat roof near where she is imprisoned. There are two small windows at the top of the storeroom. They are out of reach of my head, or else I would risk speaking with her; but your small, agile . . . um . . . friend can climb up to them and tell the Princess of my plan."

Lyn felt herself grow cold. Why, oh why, wasn't Greg here? He was so athletic; but then, he would be in danger.

"All speed possible is necessary for I must do this swiftly if I am to be at my guard post on time."

Lyn felt everyone's eyes on her and heard the Captain mutter, "If only the King were here."

The Master looked at her. "What do you say, Child from Earth? Think well, the decision is yours."

She had to go, she knew it; and even in a way, was glad that she had to be the one taking the risk, not Greg. She stood up, still cold and trembling, and swallowed hard. The Master's deep eyes were looking down at her. She beckoned, and he bent down his head until she could speak in his ear. "Do you think he is telling the truth?"

"Can you not see the reflection of the Blue Road in his eyes, Child from Earth? His plan may fail, but his heart will be true to what he has learned from looking on the Blue Road."

That was only partly reassuring, Lyn thought ruefully. Still, she managed to say, "I will go."

"I will take you on my back to the Mount," said the Dark Dragon. "There is little chance of our being seen. On the Mount I have hidden a carrying basket. In that I will take you to the palace."

"But you Dark Dragons never use carrying baskets," objected an elderly dragon.

"Now that we have discovered how useful they are, we do," said the warrior. "We all have them."

"What about the Princess' Nurse? She cannot be left behind; she would be slain," said the Captain.

"I shall warn her. She works in the kitchen; it will be easy to speak with her. She is free; they know she will not leave the Princess."

Lyn climbed onto Ralawir's back quickly to keep herself from thinking about what was ahead. He rose gently as the Captain had warned him to fly slowly and carefully and not to swerve suddenly. The Captain flew part of the way to the Mount with

168

them and then they went on alone. At the Mount, Ralawir pulled a large carrying basket from where he had hidden it. It was partly full of a vegetable called pelen which Lyn had seen being cooked. Pelen is like huge celery stalks at least four feet long and has a strong and unpleasant odor.

"Get in there," he said. "When I drop down it will be on the flat roof. Do not speak until you are by the window."

"Let me take out these stalks," Lyn said. "They smell so strong."

"No, they will hide you, and their odor will cover yours should anyone come close. My friends know I am fond of pelen, and they will think nothing of my having a basket full of it."

Lyn crawled in, and Ralawir flew off. Soon she heard a voice greet him, and the wingbeats of another dragon came alongside them as she crouched down, half-asphyxiated in the basket. Then they were alone again. She heard Ralawir answer the challenge of the tower guard and then felt him land.

"Get out quietly, and keep your head low," he said as he tipped the basket on its side. She crawled out, pulling several of the long stalks with her, and gathered by the dark outlines above her that they were on the small roof Ralawir had mentioned.

"Over there," he murmured, shoving her gently towards a wall. "Climb up that. The windows are in the wall beyond."

Lyn felt her way to the wall, thankful that Ralawir was between her and the drop to the stone courtyard. The top of the wall was above her head, but it was covered with centuries-old vines whose stems she could feel were as thick as her wrist. It was not hard to scramble to the top, but every rustle she made sent her heart into her throat. A few feet beyond rose another and higher wall. She crept on her hands and knees towards it and felt around for the windows. They were only a couple of feet above the roof.

She listened and thought she heard breathing. She stuck her head in through an opening and called down softly, "Edrina! Edrina!"

A heavy rustling followed, and then she heard Edrina's voice at the window. "Who is it?"

"Lyn."

She heard Edrina gasp with astonishment, and from the noises below she gathered the others were also getting up and coming close.

Lyn hastily whispered Ralawir's plan and then said, "There is only one thing he demands of you. He demands you to swear by the Blue Road, that whatever happens, you will not pause or turn back but will fly as fast as you can towards the Green Dragons' patrol line. If you are pursued, he says, let the young ones scatter and drop down and hide in the forests. But you must give your oath to keep on, for the pursuers will not care about the others, only you."

Edrina hesitated. "I would hate to abandon these children." She thought for a moment.

From around her came pathetic, whispered entreaties: "Please say yes, please!"

"Very well," she said. "Tell the brave Ralawir that I swear by the Blue Road that no matter what happens, I shall neither turn back nor pause."

"Farewell," Lyn whispered and started creeping back. The sound of a voice hailing Ralawir made her flatten frantically on the roof. Fortunately, Ralawir's friend had hopped up beside him instead of dropping down.

"I am tired," said the other dragon. "I have flown far today into our land bearing the King's command that all be here by early afternoon tomorrow when he intends to wed the Princess Edrina."

"Is it certain she will wed him?" said Ralawir. Lyn heard him take a stalk of pelen out of the basket and start chewing it.

"If she refuses, our King is certain she will quickly change her mind when she sees the other captives being torn to pieces in front of her, when her consent would save them."

Lyn shuddered so hard she feared the other dragon would hear. Ralawir merely took another stalk and kept on chewing.

"Ralawir, how can you stand eating pelen raw, and with me right beside you, too? You know how I hate it!" With a great flap of his wings, the dragon indignantly flew off.

Lyn slid over the edge and climbed down the ivy, landing on Ralawir at the bottom. "Into the basket," he said, pushing it towards her. She crawled in head first. He slipped his head through the strap and took off before she had time to right herself. She struggled into a sitting position, so that she could at least partly breathe.

Ralawir flew steadily.

"Can I put my head out?" she begged after a while in a whisper. "I am almost suffocated."

He gave a slight chuckle. "You do not like pelen either? Yes, we are almost at the Mount."

Even though the clouded sky made it hard for her to see ahead, she could sense the Mount as they approached. Ralawir circled and landed almost exactly at the place from where they had taken off. He tipped the basket over, and she crawled out and stood up. The Captain had promised that he and the others would be waiting to carry her back. She saw nothing, but Ralawir did.

"Who is there?" he asked.

"It is I, Damor the King. Ralawir, I thank you for your great heart and your valor in attempting to rescue my sister, the Princess. When you return with her, should you wish to remain, you will be welcomed as a friend and held in honor among us."

"I thank you, King Damor. Having looked upon your Blue Road, I would indeed find it hard not to look on it again. But who knows what the hours of this night may bring? Farewell. I must make haste to reach my post on time." And he was in the air before Lyn had time to add her thanks to Damor's.

Lyn told them what had happened and the oath Ralawir had made the Princess swear.

"He fears for her," Damor said, "and so do I."

Damor ordered a dragon to take Lyn to the base closest to the patrol lines while he, the Captain, and several warriors remained hidden on the Mount. The sky was clearing and from there they could watch for the escaping dragons and intercept and attack any pursuers.

There was nothing for those at the base to do except wait and wait and wait. No one felt like telling stories. Everyone except the Master was restless. He lay silently. Lyn sat beside him and was comforted by his very quietness. Another comfort was the arrival of Greg who had been sent for by Damor. Katanga was with him.

A faint pre-dawn gray was touching the summer sky and the camp fires were dying, when cries of welcome rang out overhead and Edrina dropped down with Damor beside her. She was weeping so bitterly she could barely acknowledge the joyful greetings around her. It was a while before she could speak. In the meantime a warrior shepherded down three youngsters, two dragons and a dragoness. They huddled together looking utterly woebegone.

At last Edrina said, "Forgive me for weeping when you are rejoicing over our escape. I, too, rejoice, but I must also grieve.

"The brave Ralawir's plan worked perfectly. At his signal we went out through the trees where Nurse joined us. At another signal we took flight and had gone but a short distance when a cry rang out behind us. We fled with all speed. Glancing back, I saw we were pursued by two dragons who were gaining on us. Ralawir called to me, 'Remember your oath, Princess!' I in turn called to the young ones to scatter. Again I looked. Ralawir had turned back to stop them and . . . and . . ." She began to weep again. "Nurse had turned back also. Then my heart failed; I nearly broke my oath. When I looked again, Nurse was falling – I do not know how she held off that warrior so long – and both warriors were attacking Ralawir. I think he, too, fell;

then Damor and my own were around me, and so we reached safety."

There was a long silence. Finally, the Master said, "Do not grieve, Princess Edrina, for they went to the Blue Road rejoicing that they had given their lives for you."

"Ralawir, too?" Lyn asked.

"Most surely." The Master lifted his voice. "Ever remember down the ages in your tales, O Green Dragons, the Dark warrior, Ralawir, who had the courage to look upon the Blue Road and was true to what it taught him."

After the rejoicing over the Princess' return had quieted a little, Damor summoned the three young-sters to him. They were all what the dragons call older children, that is, in their thirties. They had remained in the same place where they had landed, not daring to move and looking more and more miserable. None of them had armbands. Where their armbands had been were deep gashes.

"What have you to say for yourselves?" Damor sternly demanded.

"Please forgive us," begged the two elder ones, a dragon and the dragoness. The youngest, a dragon, said nothing, only wept.

"Why did you take off your armbands?" Damor continued, still sternly.

Edrina spoke up quickly. "That, my brother, is not their fault. They did not want to, but were bul-lied and struck and threatened with torture until they gave in. Then their arms were torn in punish-ment for having worn them. I witnessed this myself. Last night when we were imprisoned together, there was nothing they grieved for more, except their parents, than the loss of their armbands. Besides, my brother, we are all very hungry as we have not had anything to eat since the day before yesterday."

"The Princess is on their side," said the dragon beside Lyn with a slight chuckle, and added, "I think the King is also, only he feels they need a reprimand."

Damor questioned them. The oldest dragon was their spokesman. He admitted frankly that he, like the other young dragons, had followed Wondan because he was bored and a visit to the Dark Dragons had promised excitement. It was easy to see he was the leader and had persuaded the others to go with him. Nor did he deny it. Everything had seemed pleasant and fun at first and they had been greatly commended for being able to think independently and to cast off the foolish restrictions of the Green Dragons' laws. The treatment of the past few days had rudely awakened him and left him hating the Dark Dragons and their ways, along with being bewildered and confused.

He bravely acknowledged himself in the wrong. They all did, and begged for pardon and asked for another chance. The little group looked apprehensively at the King.

"Who are your parents?" Damor asked the leader.

"I am his father," said one of the warriors present, "and I am ashamed of him. My wife and I have always gone faithfully to the Master and sent him as well."

"That is true," said the Master. "They have been

excellent parents, but when their son came he was not attentive. The old Master reproved him for it several times."

The youngster dropped his head and said apologetically, "He was so old and took so long to say anything that I grew tired listening, though I knew I should."

Damor spoke kindly but seriously, then told them to go and have their wounds treated and to get a meal. When rested, they were to return to their families. After they had recovered they must do whatever the Master told them. "As for you," he said to the young dragon's father, "now is the time above all when he needs you to be a true father to him."

The warrior did not need to do much thinking about that. He touched his son gently with his head and said, "Your mother and I rejoice to have you back again. Come with me, my son. Tomorrow we shall speak about this matter."

Later in the morning, Lyn was wandering around the base and saw the young dragon, his arm bound in curative leaves, fast asleep with his head pillowed against his father.

When told, Damor chuckled, "It is good to have them back."

"But if he had such good parents, how did he go astray?" asked Greg.

"He is more intelligent and active than they and he longed for excitement as most do at that age. Had all been as it should have been in this land, he would undoubtedly have passed safely to maturity of thought and heart; instead he was easy prey to

Wondan's promises of an exciting freedom."

"Now he will be all right, won't he?" Lyn asked anxiously.

"The choice is still his to make, but I think he will never forget this bitter lesson and will one day be a dragon that his parents can be proud of."

CHAPTER 10
In the Shed

With Edrina safe, the twins expected Damor and the Captain to intensify the drive to push the Dark Dragons back to their own country. This did not happen. Several quiet days followed. Damor sent Edrina to stay with an aunt and recover from the effects of her imprisonment. A few raids took place. In one of them Damor received a nasty though not serious wound and was grounded for a couple of days. Nothing tries the patience of a dragon as much as being grounded. Damor, however, did not take out his impatience on those around him and in a few days was able to fly again.

"Aren't you going to attack them now, good and hard?" asked Greg, thinking of modern warfare methods. "Don't you want to drive them out before winter sets in?"

"Most certainly. Look." He took them up. "See where our lines are now?"

"Why, they are much farther away!" exclaimed Lyn, as she saw the patrol lines beyond the base of the Mount.

"Yes. We moved up last night and found no Dark warriors where we expected them to be. Why they have been removed, I do not know. But we can guess. We found out much from Edrina, and much more from all the young dragons who saw far more

178

than the Dark ones knew or would have liked.

"Many of the Dark warriors are discontented. They do not like having to stay on guard constantly as they must do if they want to hold what they have taken. It is only the power of their King that keeps them here. Should he fall, we think it would be easy to drive them back without great resistance. The Captain' has challenged the King several times to a wing-to-wing combat, but he has not answered and that surprises us for, as you know, he is a mighty warrior. We suspect he is either planning a direct attack of some kind or trying to quiet the unrest among his own."

"But if he falls, how can you be sure his heir will not continue the war?" Greg asked.

"He has three sons. The eldest is a good enough warrior but prefers to spend his time among admiring dragonesses. His second son is bold and fierce like his father and envies his elder brother, who will become King. The brothers hate each other, and their father's death would undoubtedly throw them into conflict. The eldest would have to withdraw warriors from this land to strengthen his side. He would also have to do it promptly, for many of the warriors prefer his brother."

"What about the third son?" asked Lyn.

"He is but a child."

"So you are waiting to see what happens while getting closer and closer to the palace and surrounding it?"

"We will not surround it, but instead will leave open the side towards their land so they can escape. If we surround it, they would fight, and fight desperately, 'with their tails to the wall' as we say. As you know they are fierce warriors, and many of ours would be slain. Many of theirs, too, but they have already lost more than we have, and once back in their own land it is not likely they will try to attack us again for many a long passing. Not even the second brother, though his joy is in fighting.

"That is why the Captain is trying to engage the King in single combat. We are also keeping close watch in the north and south for fear, as I said, that their King is planning a direct attack."

"I do not think he will do that," said the Captain who had come up. "He is too clever a warrior, unless he tries to quell his warriors' restlessness by such means. Farewell. I go searching for him now." He called to a warrior to accompany him and flew off.

So the summer became late summer and still nothing decisive happened. Greg's and Lyn's hands were more in demand than ever, since there were so many fruits and berries to be harvested for the winter. They picked and picked and, as Damor's warriors moved forward, they moved with them into new warm fields and groves.

Greg was surprised at his sister's energy and perseverance in the work. Back home, he was the one who did his share of the household tasks thoroughly, if not enthusiastically. Lyn was inclined to cut corners and leave things half done. When he commented on this she said, "I keep thinking of the Master's Do's and Don'ts, and he's right – the Do's are the most important."

"I have been thinking about that myself," he

said. They both laughed.

"We'll end up by having long thinking silences in the middle of conversations like the dragons, and then what will people at home say!" said Lyn, and they laughed again.

A reddish-yellow fruit the size of an apple that grew on low bushes was especially popular with the dragons. One morning a dragoness took them to a new area just behind the lines which was full of bushes, heavy with ripe fruit, and in no time they were down to their last basket. As it was still early they asked the dragoness to take their full baskets and bring them some more. She flew off and they went on busily picking. Soon they heard the beat of wings.

"That was fast flying," commented Greg. "I thought we would have this basket filled before she came back."

Lyn glanced up casually and screamed with terror. "Dark Dragons! Run!" Two of the enemy were dropping down on them.

They dashed towards the nearest trees, but it was too late. Before they got anywhere near them, each was caught up by a dragon. Lyn shrieked and shrieked, hoping a Green Dragon would hear her, but if one did, the Dark Dragons had too much of a head start. Greg twisted and hit at the forelegs that grasped him, but the dragon squeezed him so tightly that he too yelled, but in pain.

"Stop that, both of you," growled the one who held Greg, "or we'll squeeze tighter until you do."

Helplessly they saw they were being carried towards the palace. Their captors did not land in front on the terrace, however, or even in the courtyard where they had been taken on the day of their arrival, but near a shed where several dragons were lolling around a large bowl of some kind of drink.

"Where is the King?" demanded Lyn's captor.

"Off somewhere. He said he would be back this afternoon. What have you got there?" said one of the dragons.

"Prisoners. We slipped right through Damor's patrols. They are getting careless of late and the warriors were so far apart we easily went between them, caught these two and were gone before they could get near us."

"Odd-looking things they are," commented another dragon.

"They fit the description Magior gave of those strangers, children from some place . . . Earth, he called it. He said they stole the Coronation Collars. Did you steal them?" he demanded, turning fiercely on Greg.

Greg decided the only thing to do was to try to bluff. "I'm not going to say anything until I see your King," he said as boldly as he could, trying to play for time.

"Answer me like that, will you?" snarled the dragon, knocking him over with a blow of his head.

"Better not harm him before the King comes," cautioned the dragon who had first spoken. "He has been in a raging mood since the Princess escaped. Did you know he was so furious when he found it out, he slew the dragoness who told him, and he was particularly fond of her? If these prisoners are the ones who stole the jewels, he will probably tear them to pieces."

"Then be sorry afterwards, when he cools down, that he did not keep them as hostages or for ransom," said the third dragon. They all chuckled harshly at this last remark. The King's ways were well known to them. But all this was far from reassuring to the children. Lyn was terrified, and Greg was not far from it, though both tried not to show it.

"What shall we do with them in the meantime?" said Greg's dragon. He seemed undecided. "Perhaps I should take them into the palace."

"Shove them into that shed and join us in finishing this bowl," said another of the lolling dragons. That decided the children's captors. They were pushed into the shed, the door closed behind them, and the two dragons joined their friends around the enormous bowl.

Coming as they did from the sunlight into the dark, they could see nothing at first. "What are we going to do now?" said Lyn, trying to keep her voice from shaking, and grateful that Greg could not see her face in the dark.

"I don't know. Let's try to think. Perhaps we can make their King believe we are important enough to keep us as hostages." Greg said this to keep their spirits up because he did not want to think what would happen to them if the Dark King did not want to keep them as prisoners.

The door had a large crack in it and Greg peered through. He could see the dragons noisily dipping their smaller bowls into the big one and settling down to drink. The door was right in front of them. There was no use even thinking of escaping that way.

He still had his eye against the hole when Lyn whispered excitedly, "Look!" While he was watching, her eyes had become accustomed to the dim light and she had been examining the shed. It was a storage shed of some kind, full of baskets and odds and ends. The walls were high and windowless, but right under the roof were small openings, evidently for ventilation in order to keep the shed and its contents from becoming musty. The openings were long and narrow, mere slits to a dragon.

"I think we could squeeze through the back one," Lyn said.

"Maybe we could, but how do we get up there?" He went over to the back and looked up. "Anyway, there are probably dragons lying all around and they would see us."

They both thought. "I have it," said Lyn. "We can pile the baskets in a pyramid and climb up them."

"Great idea, Lyn," Greg whispered back excitedly. "It's our only chance. Let's try, but remember the dragons have terribly keen hearing."

As quietly as they could, they first cleared the back wall of the tangle of baskets, then laid a row of five tall baskets along the bottom, then four on top of them, then three, then two.

Greg was on the top. "Hand me another."

"That's all. Can we possibly make it?" They were short one basket and there was a good six feet between the top of the baskets and the opening.

"I can pile the last two baskets on top of each other, leaving just enough room to step up. There, now I think I can make it." He climbed down. "We must have a way to get down on the other side."

He took out his knife, which had already come in handy in innumerable ways, and cut several of the carrying straps from the lower baskets. He tied them together into one long strap and wrapped it around his waist.

"Let me go first," he said. "Then I can pull you up if you can't get on top of the last two baskets."

He cautiously climbed up the first two steps of the pyramid while Lyn did her best to steady the structure. Beyond that, she could barely reach and the upper rows of baskets swayed and creaked as he crawled up them.

"Can you do it?" Lyn whispered anxiously.

"I think so, but there is nothing to hang on to. The wall is smooth and if I lean against it, the whole pile sways outwards, and if I don't, I sway outwards."

Lyn could feel the pyramid wobble as Greg climbed higher and did not dare think what would happen to him . . . or to her if it tumbled down.

"I'm at the top," came Greg's muffled voice. His head was pressed against the highest of the last two baskets that were piled on top of each other as he tried to get a foothold without upsetting them.

"I can reach the opening now," he called down softly, "but it is terribly narrow and a jump will upset everything."

He eased himself up gently inch by inch until he was standing on top of the unsteady basket. His head and shoulders were level with the top of the wall and he could see the area behind the shed.

About fifty feet back was the edge of the woods that surrounded the palace grounds. No dragons were in sight.

He squeezed himself into the space under the roof and lay on top of the wall straddling it. What had seemed easy from below was difficult to execute. By dangerously wiggling this way and that – he nearly fell off at one moment – and pulling with one hand while holding on with the other, he managed to unwind the strap from his waist. He looped it around a roof support, then told Lyn to start up.

Cautiously she crept up the mound, wishing she had gone first since the last basket, which had been pushed slightly out of place by Greg's last heave, wobbled more than ever.

"I can't possibly get on top of those two baskets," she panted after several futile tries. "I'll just push the top one off."

"Here, get hold of this strap and try to pull yourself up. I'll grab your arm as soon as I can."

Lyn felt along the wall and found the strap. With a scramble she got within reach of his hand. He heaved as hard as he could from his cramped position. Lyn made it to the top of the baskets, and two things happened at once. She felt the basket start to give way, and letting go of the strap managed to get her arms over the edge just before the basket rolled down the pile, leaving her feet kicking in the air. The sudden loosening of the tension on the strap threw Greg off balance, and he fell outwards, still hanging to the strap which jerked him sharply to a stop. He slid the rest of the way to the ground, burning his hands and scraping his knuckles badly against the wall, but landing unhurt.

Lyn with a violent heave and struggle got into a safe position on top of the wall. The ground looked far away, but with the help of the strap she got down more easily than Greg had, because he dug his heels in and held the strap firmly a little away from the wall. As soon as she was down, Greg crawled towards the trees, creeping through the long grass with Lyn behind him, both afraid that a cracking branch would give them away. Once they were well among the trees they stood up and went deeper into the woods, slowly at first and then when out of earshot as quickly as they could. They came to a Dragon-Cousin path.

"We'd go much faster if we followed this, but which way is best?" said Lyn looking in each direction.

Greg hesitated. "Let's try to the right. We can only guess. Let me go ahead. I know how fast you can go." They ran down the path until they came to a river.

"We're behind the palace," said Lyn. "Look, over there is one of the ruined bridges. And I can just see part of a tower. Let's get away from here as fast as we can."

"We must try to head for the sea," said Greg as they ran back into the forest. "After that we can go south keeping to the forests until we get to our patrol line."

They skirted the palace grounds in a wide circle, staying always in the deepest part of the woods and avoiding any open places. Fortunately, at first there was a Dragon-Cousin path that went in the direction they wanted to go, and when it turned off they went through the woods again. Sometimes they had to find a way around or through heavy undergrowth, but mostly they made good time.

"Damor must be hunting for us now," they said to encourage each other, and, "Did anyone see us being carried off?" was the question they asked over and over.

"I'm sure he will guess what's happened even if the dragoness didn't see us being carried off. Maybe the patrol saw it, but were too far off to do anything," said Greg.

"But even if they saw us, what can Damor do?" worried Lyn. "We must get to him even if we have to walk all night."

The dragons' noontime resting period was over and they wondered what was going to happen.

"How long do you think it will be before they discover we are gone?"

"Until the Dark King comes, I suppose."

"Do you think the dragons will dare tell their King about capturing us when they find we've escaped? Or will they come hunting us first?" wondered Lyn, when they had put a good distance between themselves and the palace.

Greg could not help laughing. "I would like to see their faces when they open the door and find the shed empty."

They went on steadily towards the east, keeping the afternoon sun behind them as best they could, but after a while the sky clouded over and they could only guess at their direction. What made it more difficult was their having to go around irregularly shaped meadows and glades instead of crossing them. Ahead loomed foothills. Greg remembered there being foothills between the palace and the sea. Lyn didn't think there were any.

"Well," said Greg, "since we are near these foothills, let's climb up them a little way. We'll be able to look over the valley without being seen. Maybe we can see the sun from there."

"At least we'll see the Mount. Then we'll know where we are and how much farther we have to go. It can't be terribly far."

They turned towards the foothills and walked rapidly through a forest whose trees were huge but which had little undergrowth. Lyn was ahead and as she came to a clearing she stopped so abruptly that Greg ran into her. They were back in the glade with the strange Door.

They stood looking at it.

At last Lyn said, "Does this mean we are supposed to go back through it now?"

"If we go through it, can we come back? I don't want to leave without Damor knowing we're all right."

Lyn thought hard. "The old King said we should go back when we must. But this doesn't seem like a *must* time, does it?"

"You go, Lyn. After all, the Dark Dragons are holding this area and it's dangerous to be here."

"I won't," she said fiercely. "I won't. I'm not going without you. And I'm certainly staying if we can still help Damor."

"All right. At least we know now more or less where we are and where the sea is. We'll have to keep to the forests the way the Dragon-Cousins do and sooner or later we'll be far enough south. It shouldn't take us more than a day."

"I'm glad we had a big breakfast, though we'll probably find enough fruit to keep us going," said Lyn. "And look how dark the sky is getting. If it rains hard there is much less chance of their trying to catch us. Dragons so hate to fly in heavy rains."

Feeling much more cheerful with the foothills at their back, they went into the forest again. They had only gone a short distance when they came to a clearing and were about to go around well under the trees and out of sight of the sky when they heard wings.

"Stay here," said Greg. "I'm going to reconnoiter."

"I'm coming too."

They crept under a leafy thicket at the edge of the clearing and looked up. At first they saw nothing, then a Dark Dragon swept past but too far away from them to see if they could recognize one of their captors.

"He's looking for us; I'm sure he is," whispered Lyn. "See how his head is going back and forth as though searching the ground, and he is angry. See how much smoke and flame he is making."

"If so, he'll turn at some point and come back. Let's wait and see."

Nothing happened and they were about to stand up when they heard the wingbeats again. They lay absolutely still so as not to move a telltale leaf. As the dragon passed this time, almost directly overhead, they could see him plainly. Across his chest were the terrible double "S" scars. It was the Dark King, and he was hunting for them.

CHAPTER 11
The Dark King

They crept back into the forest and sat there shaking.

"Let's wait until we are sure he is far away," said Lyn. "I don't like the idea of moving even a leaf when he's around; he might spot it."

"Nor do I," Greg was beginning, then stopped abruptly and thought hard. "I've got it! We can help Damor and the Green Dragons. Remember what he said would happen if the Dark King fell?"

"Yes, that it would almost certainly end the war and the Dark Dragons' occupation of this land. But what about it?" Lyn asked.

"And remember what David and Laura told us? Besides, we've heard it a dozen times in the dragons' stories, that for us the Forbidden Door opens to our own time, but for the Dragons it opens back to the times when the knights were around killing dragons, and they never return."

"Yes, but I still don't see what you're driving at."

Greg went on excitedly. "The dragons aren't terribly fast on the ground, not what I call fast. If I let the Dark King see me in that clearing we were just in and entice him to drop down and chase me, I'm certain I can beat him in a sprint to the Door. He'll be so furious he's bound to try to follow me through it. Then I'll be in the cave and he'll be way back with the knights."

Lyn stared at him open-mouthed. "It's too dangerous! You might be killed! Suppose you tripped?"

"Don't worry, I won't. I've run over much rougher terrain than this in cross-country races."

"But suppose the Door doesn't work that way this time, and he came into the cave after us? Laura and David found Nimeon in the cave," objected Lyn.

That was an unpleasant thought.

"Nimeon was forced to go through the Door. All the others went of their own accord. But if that does happen, we'll dash into the ocean with Laura and David. He can't get us there."

"What would happen? Suppose he flew all over England!"

"What a field day the journalists would have! Just imagine the headlines: 'Dragon seen over London'," said Greg.

Frightened as they were, they laughed at the picture.

"Are you certain the Door isn't too far away from the clearing, and what shall I do while you are running?" Lyn continued anxiously. She didn't like Greg's plan one little bit.

"Go towards the Door right now and stop the moment you can see it clearly; then I'll know exactly where to run."

Lyn hurried through the trees. Only a short distance away she found a large tree trunk had blocked their view of the hillside, the glade and the Door. She waved and ran back. "You can see the Door easily from that tree. It's not far."

"All right. Go almost to the edge of the glade but keep out of sight of the sky. When you hear me call, you'll know he's dropping down. Run through the Door and hold it open for me. Then let go of it the instant I dash through."

Greg went back to the clearing and from under the trees watched the sky. He wanted to be certain it was the Dark King who fell into his trap. When he saw the great dark wings and scarred chest, he stepped out as though walking into the clearing. The King gave a harsh, triumphant cry. Greg yelled a warning, half saw the dragon close its wings, and leapt into the forest as the Dark King landed with an earthquaking thud.

He raced confidently ahead with the dragon crashing through the forest after him. Greg, however, had made two miscalculations. He had never seen how fast a dragon can travel for a short distance in half-bounding leaps, and he had forgotten how far a dragon can shoot his flame. Luckily, not as far when bounding over land as in the air – they get too winded – but far enough. As Greg ducked around the large tree, a hot breath touched one shoulder. Ahead was the Door with Lyn beside it. He saw her dart through and hold it open. He heard the Dark King come around the tree, and he ran as he had never run in any race. He tore across the glade. As he reached the Door, the tip of a fiery blast hit him between the shoulders. He leaped through, it swung shut, and he was in the cave.

"Quick! Into the ocean!" he yelled, dragging David who was nearest him, while Lyn pulled a bewildered Laura along. They splashed into the

194

shallows, then stopped. Nothing happened. No dragon came hurtling out of the cave. Standing up to their knees in the sea, Greg and Lyn explained what they were afraid might happen.

"A Dark Dragon King!" cried David. "That was a clever trick! But I think we are safe. If he went through the Door, he's with the knights."

"And I hope he meets one right away," said Greg moving his shoulders. They felt very sore.

"Your shirt is scorched. The back of your neck looks as though you have a dreadful sunburn," said Laura.

"It feels like it!"

They waded back to the beach and went carefully and cautiously into the cave. The Door was still there and after a bit the twins were anxious to find out what had happened.

"You stand back, Lyn," Greg ordered. "I'm going to open the Door and see if he is there. If I yell, jump into the water."

"No, I won't," retorted Lyn. "I'm going to see what happened also."

Greg pushed the Door open a crack and both of them peered through. "I don't see anything, Lyn, do you? No sign of a dragon, and it has started to rain."

"I don't see anything either, but it might be a trick, with him hiding somewhere nearby."

Greg pushed the Door a little farther, and it swung open though he tried to hold it back. He stuck his head through and looked all around, in the forest, on the slopes above. No dragon. "Come on, Lyn," he said, and they went into the glade. The

Door shut behind them.

They examined the glade but there was nothing to show whether the King had gone through the Door or had flown off.

"Let's get under cover. I'll feel safer," said Lyn, putting her words into action. "Now we'll have to get to Damor as fast as we can so as to let him know what may have happened."

In their haste to get away from that dangerous place, they completely forgot their plan of climbing part way up the foothills so as to see where they were. By the time they remembered, they were deep in the forest; so they headed in what they thought was a southerly direction, always making a wide circle around all open areas, even small ones. A shallow, slow-moving river crossed their path. They carefully searched the sky above it for any sign of dragons, then dashed across and into the trees on the farther side without stopping to take off their shoes.

"I think that's the same river we saw the first day in the meadow where I stepped on the warrior's tail," said Lyn.

"I think you're right, it is about the same distance from the Door. If so, we're headed in the right direction. I remember noticing that it flowed from east to west."

Much encouraged, they trudged on. The rain stopped but the sun remained obstinately hidden. A couple of hours later, after crossing the fourth loop of the same river, they realized they had no idea in which direction they were going. The next meadow they came to was a large one, and on one side it ended at the base of a hill. They were debating whether to go around or over the hill when Greg noticed the roof of a dragon house tucked as usual among the trees. They at once decided to climb up to it, keeping hidden, and see if there were any signs of Green Dragons.

"I don't think we're anywhere near Damor's patrol lines, but we just might be," said Greg.

"Then we could get a ride on a friendly dragon. I'm dead tired," said Lyn wearily.

Not a sign of life greeted them as they peered around some bushes at the houses. They ventured in a little nearer, still keeping under the trees so as not to be seen from the sky. Near the first house, Lyn stopped with a cry.

"Look down there," she said, pointing to the meadow. Below them lay the shallow, warm bowl of a nursery. The deep, sandy floor was raked with gashes from one end to the other showing a terrific struggle had taken place. "That must be the nursery Damor told us was attacked by the Dark Dragons the day of their invasion. Remember how infuriated the Green warriors were when they heard that not only had one of their nurseries with their unhatched eggs been destroyed, but also the families living nearby had been slaughtered? These must be their homes."

Greg nodded uneasily. "Wasn't that nursery near the palace? If so, we've been going in a circle. Let's get away from here."

They looked into a house as they went by. It was the saddest sight they had ever seen, and Lyn could not help crying, while Greg bit his lip hard. A dragoness mother had been preparing a meal; the pots were on the long-cold stove, and a little crib was overturned and its bedding scattered.

They were so distressed they forgot the threat from the skies and went over to the next house without keeping under the trees. On coming out they heard the sound of wings and before they could run anywhere, a dragon dropped down beside them. It was Tormagon, the young warrior with whom Greg had argued unsuccessfully.

"Tormagon!" they shouted joyfully. Lyn hugged him in relief.

He was equally glad to see them, but before they could ask a question, "Wait!" he cried and shot up into the air again. He called out loudly, but they were unable to make out what he was saying.

Down he dropped again. "I was calling to the guard on the palace tower to tell the King you are here."

"The palace! The King!" they cried in surprise.

"Yes, the palace is only a short distance away on the other side of this hill and the King is on the terrace. I saw him there a few moments ago."

He did not have time to say more before half a dozen dragons swept over the hill. The sky was clearing, and Damor's ruby collar sparkled in the sun; then he was down beside them. With him were the Captain, several warriors, and a couple of dragonesses.

What rejoicings there were! Lyn hugged Damor and then, in her excitement, all the dragons. The next moment Edrina landed and there were more hugs by Lyn and Greg and gentle head taps from the dragons.

"Are you really back at the palace, Damor?" cried Greg. "How did you manage to recapture it in such a short time?"

"Short time?" said Damor with a chuckle. "You two have been gone eighteen days. And during those eighteen days, the Dark Dragons have been driven out, our warriors are back in their garrisons along the border, and the families who live hereabouts and in the north have returned to their homes."

All the dragons chuckled at the twins' exclamations of surprise.

"Did the Dark King really never come back?" asked Lyn. She was standing by Damor and hugging him every now and then.

"Never! We knew that you, our brave, brave friends, led him through the Forbidden Door to his doom."

"We tried, or rather Greg did. I just held the Door open so Greg could get through it faster. But how did you know?"

"Remember I told you the Captain was seeking to engage the King in a wing-to-wing combat? That day he, with a companion, was searching the skies. He spied the King and sped to meet him. The King dropped down into the forest calling out his battle cry, and as the Captain flew over, he saw him disappearing into the forest. He followed him by the movement of the trees below. He saw you, Greg, running through the Forbidden Door. A moment later the Dark King broke out of the forest and hurled himself after you. The Captain circled above

199

for a while. No one came forth so he left. He dared fly close to the palace where he called to a warrior that his King had rashly gone through the Forbidden Door and would never return. The Dark warrior was so astonished, he asked if the stories about the Door were really true. 'Aye,' the Captain replied, 'make haste and tell his son. If you are the first, he may reward you!'

"The warrior must have done what the Captain suggested, for though we saw some searching for the King, it was half-hearted. None cared to go anywhere near the Door. During the next two days we saw many comings and goings, and more goings than comings. On the third day we judged the time ripe and attacked the palace. Only," there was much chuckling from the warriors present, "there was nothing to attack, not even a guard on the tower. All we found were three dragons and two dragonesses feasting in the courtyard. One of the dragonesses was wearing Edrina's gold collar. They took to flight when they saw us, and when the Captain ordered the dragoness to give back the collar, she threw it at his head. We let them go except for one warrior whom we drove to the ground, but released after he had given us what news he had.

"The Dark King's two older sons were fighting. Both of them had summoned the warriors still in our land to their cause. Some went to one son, some to the other. So it was no great feat to drive out the few Dark Dragons still remaining here; only some eight or ten who had found our houses to their liking. By that night, our warriors were back in their garrisons patrolling the whole border and our land was our own again!"

"Hoorah! Hoorah!" shouted the twins.

"Much remains to be done," continued Damor. "Damaged fields and flocks must be restored, and the scars to our way of life healed. But they are healing, and already we are one in heart as I have never before seen."

"What the King says is true," said the Captain, "and our new spirit will be sealed by his Solemn Coronation two days hence."

"I'm so glad we came back in time for that," cried Lyn, clapping her hands.

"Yes, and we'll see the Coronation Collars worn in the proper way instead of around our waists," said Greg, laughing.

"What happened to Magior?" was Greg's next question.

"The same dragon we captured told us that it was not likely he would get any of the rewards the old King promised him for his treachery. He is trying to ingratiate himself with the elder of the warring brothers and has been given a small, ignominious position that no Dark Dragon wants and is treated with contempt. Very likely he will either be slain, for they do not trust him, or else he will sink lower and lower until he ends his days in misery, tormented by the remembrance of what he threw away."

Lyn could not get the ravaged nursery and the pathetically deserted houses out of her mind. While the others talked and rejoiced, she said softly to Damor, "What will happen to that nursery? It looks so sad and lonely."

"That is one of the scars to be healed, and one of the most sorrowful. But it will be. Before winter comes, it will be remade and filled with more warm sand. Two young couples who will be married soon are going to live there, and their little ones will see the guards, the nurse and the parents coming for their new children as those before them did."

At the palace Katanga hurried out to greet them. He exclaimed over Greg's flame-reddened back and insisted on getting a soothing ointment for it which Lyn put on for him. His back did look like a case of very bad sunburn and the back of his shirt was scorched from the neck to the waist.

"Now, how am I going to explain *that* back home?" asked Greg.

Lyn laughed. "I'll wash and iron it and say I scorched it with the iron."

Greg glanced at her anxiously. They were both very truthful, and he did not want her to fib even for him.

She saw his look and laughed again. "Don't worry. I'll just turn the iron to top heat and by the time I'm finished, it will be true."

Katanga wanted to take them to see the Dragon-Cousins, most of whom were back in their houses. They passed the kitchen and looked in. There was Partemegan, cheery as ever.

"I am the Head Baker," he said, scurrying up to one of the ovens and pulling out three five-foot loaves with a pronged pole and laying them on racks to cool. "The King gave me the post as soon as I asked for it. Some day I may even be Head Cook. Who knows? Do have a bite of bread. I am invent-

ing a new recipe for the feast the day after tomorrow. I shall call it 'Coronation Bread'."

So they sat down on a table while he bustled
around and brought them dishes and bowls and
gave them a drink with large chunks of his freshly
made bread to go with it, chatting all the time.

"Nothing exciting happened on the Mount after
you left until the night that Dark warrior brought
the basket of pelen. I wondered what he was about
and kept a close watch. When I saw him arrive with
you, Lyn, on his back, I knew something was up.
Then Damor and the Captain came and told me.
Too bad that Dark warrior was slain. Not at all like
the others. Used to sit on the Mount looking at the
Blue Road.

"Anytime you want a bite of bread or anything,
just come to the kitchen," he said as they left, prais-
ing him for his new recipe.

The Dragon-Cousins were overjoyed to see them.
They were busy rebuilding communal ovens and a
few damaged buildings with bricks made in their
own principality and flown up by the dragons. They
dropped everything and crowded around Lyn and
Greg who both promised to come back whenever
they had free time to help in the building.

The news of their arrival spread, and dragons
kept dropping in (literally) the rest of the day and
the next, some bringing Dragon-Cousin friends on
their backs.

To their great delight the Master came to discuss
the Coronation ceremony with Damor. (Lyn did not
quite dare hug him.) With him were the three
youngsters who had escaped with Edrina; all were

wearing bright new armbands. The Master noticed the twins' surprise and said, "They are doing all in their power to repair the past."

The day of Damor's coronation was glorious. Only a lazy cloud floated here and there in a deep blue sky. The ceremony took place at the Field of Celebration. All traces of the earlier conflict had been removed and the gashes on the dais, made by Magior and Wondan in their fury at the Queen's denial, had been repaired.

Lyn and Greg, of course, were among the honored guests on the dais. The Queen, however, was not there.

"She did not wish to be," explained Damor. "She said that she did not want to ever set foot on the dais again. It would remind her too much of the past. There she is," he nodded a greeting to a couple right below the dais, "with the dragon she is going to marry. He has been a widower for several passings. True, it is not our custom to remarry so soon, but the Master counseled her to do so and Edrina and I also urged her to. Poor Dar-mother. She has had so much unhappiness, but I think she will be happy now. He is a fine dragon; I know him well. He will be a good husband to her and a good father to her adopted son." In answer to Lyn's question about the baby dragon, he added, "His mother, we think, was slain on account of her child, and his father fell in combat."

When all were assembled, Damor repeated the Coronation oath in which he pledged to uphold the laws of the Great One and of the Green Dragons and to do all in his power to be a faithful King.

Then the Master put the magnificent Coronation Collar on his neck. After that Damor flew the length of the field and back while the dragons cheered mightily, breathing out such great gusts of smoke in the process that it drifted in clouds across the field and set the two poor human beings to coughing and choking.

"Don't the dragons ever mind the smoke?" Greg asked the Prince of the Dragon-Cousins who was beside him.

He laughed. "It is as natural to them as breathing, and we . . . we are used to it after so many hundreds and hundreds of passings."

Then came races and exhibitions of flying and combats for everyone's entertainment. The celebrations lasted two days so that the warriors at the border posts could take turns attending with their families.

At the end of each day Damor gave a banquet at the palace. They were not sumptuous because, due to the destruction by the Dark Dragons of some of the crops and several herds, food would be sufficient but not plentiful that winter, and Damor did not wish to have more than others.

After the two days of celebration were over, Damor went to visit the few sick and elderly who were again being cared for on the Mount. Later he was going to make the rounds of the kingdom and the Dragon-Cousins' principality. Greg and Lyn went with him to the Mount. Leaving him with the sick they went to the edge of the plateau and looked out over the kingdom of the Green Dragons. An almost visible peace seemed to hang over the land.

"They are beginning over again," said Greg.

"Yes. And yet at the same time I feel as though something were coming to an end."

"Do you? I've been feeling that way too. Do you think it means the reason for our being here has ended?"

Together they looked out at the wonderful beauty of the Blue Road that stretched in front of them from the shore to the horizon.

Suddenly Lyn caught her brother's hand. "We must go home. I can't explain it, but I know we must."

Greg nodded soberly. "Yes, we must. Even though we get back to Smugglers' Cove at the same time we left it, we've been here for weeks. I keep thinking of how much of the summer I've wasted when I could have been learning from Uncle Jack."

"I know how you feel. Only with me it's other things I could do. And yet, how I hate to leave."

"I guess that is what the old King meant when he said, 'You can stay until you *must* go.' "

They ran over to Damor who was coming out of a building and told him. He was sorrowful but not surprised. "I felt the time for your going was near, for this is not your land. I grieve, but I shall always rejoice in the memory of our friendship."

The Master bade them a kind farewell. "Though," he said, "there is no real farewell for those who have looked on the Blue Road together."

His words reminded Lyn that she had never seen the Blue Road up close. "Please," she begged, "could we see the Blue Road from where it begins?"

So Damor took them down to the shore where

she and Greg stood silently for a long time looking at the wide path of luminous blue ripples that stretched before them to the horizon.

Finally Lyn turned away with a sigh. "I keep remembering Ralawir and how looking at the Blue Road changed his heart and his thoughts. I wonder what he saw there. . ."

"Everything," said Greg, as he, too, reluctantly turned away. "It holds all the answers."

Then it was goodbye to Katanga and all their friends; then onto Damor's and Edrina's backs for the last time. In a clearing not far from the Door, for Damor would not go too near it, they said a final, sad goodbye with many hugs and anxious hopes that they might one day return.

It was only a short walk through the forest to the glade and through the Door into Smugglers' Cove where Laura and David were waiting impatiently to hear what had happened. What a time they had on the beach, eating the contents of Laura's basket and their buns. They talked so long the tide rose too high for Laura and David to walk around the rocks, so they all got into the boat, and the boys did the rowing.

"Come over to Grandfather's as soon as you can," Laura said as they moored the rowboat. "He knows all about our adventures and will want to hear about yours."

They were starting up their different streets when David suddenly stopped and ran back. "I know what happened to the Dark King!" he exclaimed. "I just remembered, among Grandfather's books there is a little-known tale from King Arthur's time. It begins, 'How Sir Gawaine did slay a terrible dark dragon which had ravaged the countryside and filled all with terror, and was known by the two terrible scars on his gray chest, each of which was shaped like a great S.' I'll dig it up for you when you come over."

Just before they turned into their own street, Greg reminded Lyn about the book she had said she wanted so badly this morning, or was it weeks ago? "Or did you finally lose your purse?"

"No," she said slowly. "I didn't."

She looked longingly at the bookstore across the way, then at the little shop they were standing in front of, which had several pretty potted plants for sale in its window. Their mother loved potted plants. "I think I was *meant* not to lose it," she said, and went straight into the shop and bought the biggest plant. It took all her money.

They hurried on home. At the front door Uncle Jack was about to get into his car. Greg ran over to him.

"Uncle Jack, could I please start learning with you again?"

"Hop in," said his uncle.

Greg waved to Lyn. She waved back and, with the plant in her arms, ran into the house.

THE END